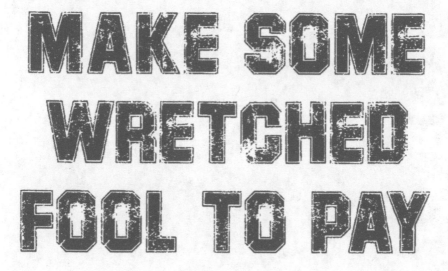

MAKE SOME WRETCHED FOOL TO PAY

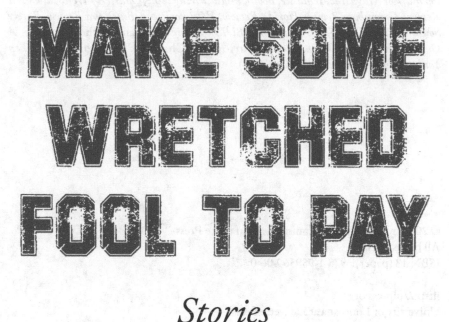

MAKE SOME WRETCHED FOOL TO PAY

Stories

Christopher Lowe

2023
UNIVERSITY OF LOUISIANA AT LAFAYETTE PRESS

Acknowledgment of Prior Publication

Pieces from this collection were originally published in slightly different form in *Permafrost Magazine*, *Yemassee*, *Booth*, *Product Magazine*, *Quarterly West*, *Yalobusha Review*, *Greensboro Review*, *Florida Review*, *WhiskeyPaper*, *Blue Lyra Review*, *Barely South Review*, *Deep South Magazine*, *BULL*, *Zahir Tales*, and in the chapbooks *A Guest of the Program* (*Iron Horse Literary Review* Chapbook Prize Series) and *When You're Down By the River* (BatCat Press).

http://ulpress.org
University of Louisiana at Lafayette Press
P.O. Box 43558
Lafayette, LA 70504-3558

cover art: "Light, A Strange Velocity," from the series *Autobiography of A Contact Sport* by Jesse Rieser

Printed in the United States
Library of Congress Cataloging-in-Publication Data

Names: Lowe, Christopher, author.
Title: Make some wretched fool to pay : stories / Christopher Lowe.
Description: Lafayette, LA : University of Louisiana at Lafayette Press, 2023.
Identifiers: LCCN 2023040802 | ISBN 9781959569060 (paperback)
Subjects: LCGFT: Short stories.
Classification: LCC PS3612.O88153 M35 2023 | DDC 813/.6--dc23/eng/20230901
LC record available at https://lccn.loc.gov/2023040802

Contents

Contents

For my mom

"... trying in vain to breathe the fire we was born in ..."
—Bruce Springsteen

Make Some Wretched Fool to Pay

Gray Ellison is my daddy's name. It's my name, too, but I try not to think of it as such. In kindergarten, when Ms. Brown called roll, I'd flinch around toward the door, expecting to see Daddy standing there. He's not a big man. Only 5'7". Whip thin. But his arms coil with muscle. He has the kind of strength that allows for prizing lug nuts from a tire with his bare hands on a bet. Ms. Brown would get to our name, and in my five-year-old head I'd hear the thunk of steel-toes on linoleum. At that point, the pivot was unavoidable. Ms. Brown probably thought I had a condition. Over time, I've learned to control that swiveling, but the impulse remains. Gray Ellison is my daddy's name, and all things being equal, I'd rather be quit of it.

We're rumbling along in my daddy's truck out toward county land, toward a bar where a man owes him money. I'm in the passenger seat, fiddling with the lock, which is coming loose. I screw it tighter, flip it up, unscrew it back loose again, until Daddy says, "You knock that thing loose, and we'll have a problem." I flip it closed and draw my hands close. I've been a fidgeter all my life, my fingers always in search of something to worry, but this evening it's worse. It's not been but three hours since I snapped my best friend's leg, since I heard his screams, felt the grip of his sweaty hand in mine as he was put on the stretcher and taken away in the ambulance.

My mother's working the night shift at the Huddle House. The place never gets crowded enough for her to make more than a few bucks a night in tips, but the money she does manage gets tight-rolled into my daddy's sock drawer. He's the breadwinner, and her tips don't alter that. Still, she leaves the two of us a couple nights a week and drives out to the highway, where the Huddle House flags down drivers with its cheap hash browns and paper steaks.

Most nights, my daddy feeds me a can of something and leaves me to the television while he drives around Luxapallila County collecting his earnings. Becoming a bookie was not a career goal for him. He'd held down a job at the tire factory in West Point until he started tending bar to make the extra money he needed to marry my mother. That's when he found his niche. Wyeth, situated southeast of Memphis and due west of Birmingham, was something of a no-man's-land at that time. When he tells this story, he grins big, tells me how the sheriff's office had run the major moonshiners out decades before. How the only drug culture in the county was a couple labs pumping out crank. The crime in Wyeth was as yet unorganized, and while individual bartenders might've taken some bets now and again, there was no formal process in place, no larger structure to kick up to. No one bookie overseeing things. "A man with enough drive can get a thing like that done," my daddy says.

We pass out of town and into county land, the shift marked by the end of a string of gas stations and pawn shops and the onset of tangling woods and catfish farms. I'm in the truck with my daddy tonight because this afternoon at football practice I snapped my best friend's fibula. I'm a linebacker, though my coach thinks if I continue to lengthen out I may end up a pass-rushing defensive end in college.

A scrimmage, the kind we always do during the afternoon heat of two-a-days. Drew came from the backfield, ball tucked. I squared up on him, stopped him short, didn't even bother to wrap him up, just speared him and drove him backward, but his foot snagged in the grass, and the momentum of my hit made a twig of his leg.

Daddy came home to find me brooding in the dark. When I told him what I'd done, told him about the way Drew had screamed, he said I was about old enough to come along with him.

Nights while my mother works, my daddy drives to each bar in the county, talks with the bartenders or bar managers or the regulars who handle things for him. He collects money, pays out earnings rarely, and threatens people when necessary.

In the evenings, I watch whatever rabbit-ears its way into our house. I'm indiscriminate in my tastes. One thing's good as another, and with only the two channels, having choice in such things seems a luxury. My daddy usually arrives home before my mother, who never gets off until hours later, long after the two of us are asleep. Some nights, he lets me stay up and watch the late movie, but more frequently, he comes through the door, glares at me, tells me it's past my bedtime, and then holes himself up in their bedroom to count his money and look over his books. There was a time when I pushed against him, against his notion of bedtime, but he ended that right quick, and since then I've not quibbled, though my friends spend their nights driving through town in shuddering pickups, windows down, mosquitos drumming smears into their late-night windshields. I go along when I can, when I get enough hate for my daddy built up to allow me to slip out the window of my room. I wait for Drew two streets over.

I rise early each morning, run my miles, ease my way through the school day, knock hell out of people at practice, and return home for the evening, for the can of chili, the few hours of broadcast television, the outgrown bedtime.

And so it's been, until tonight, this summer night in my fifteenth year, when Daddy has decided that I, too, am a dangerous man.

————

The summer is always his worst time of year. In these dog days of July, there are no sports but baseball, and even the major leagues don't offer much motivation for the gamblers of Luxapallila County. As a boy, I always associated my daddy's summer tension with the heat. I didn't understand that there was a simpler explanation. When money gets tight, his usual mild agitation turns bitter. He comes home with battered knuckles.

Out the cracked truck windows, I can smell the muddy water of the catfish ponds, the feral stench of filleted carcasses tossed to the reeds by boys poaching the farm stock. In the back of my mind, I hear the brittle snap of Drew's leg, though I try to think of something else, try to think of him running smooth, the way he does. He's been smaller than me since peewee ball, since we tucked into sleeping bags in his backyard as six-year-olds, huddling below the owls perched in the mist. He's quick, lithe, sure of each pivot, each foot-planted cut. I welcome him back to the bench after each touchdown, eye his easy smile, that loose grin that comes from never knowing anything but love. There have been moments in our lives when I've hated him for that, when I've yearned for a Disney-movie body swap—to sleep in his sheets, to wake in his room. I want to live that free, sure, but there is a part of me that wants, too, for him to know the sound of Daddy's battered knuckles rapping against the kitchen counter.

We pull into a gravel lot, a bar situated in its middle. The place is un-adorned, save for a faded Schlitz sign with the word "Hazards" on it. Back be-hind the bar is an expanse of water, the hum of oxidizers that keep the water moving and healthy for fish. I ask if Hazards is the name of the bar, and Daddy nods but doesn't speak as we pile out. I edge into the barroom behind him. There's a pool table angled into one corner with barely enough elbow room to take a decent shot. Two battered tables with folding chairs, old metal signs for beers I've never heard of, a bar top that needs sanding and a new coat of lac-quer. My daddy orders us two beers—Miller Lites—and we sit drinking them for a few minutes while the bartender putters around. On a shelf behind the bar, there's a row of model airplanes, World War II-era bombers from the look of them. They seem out of place here. Each is painted in meticulous detail. Tiny bullet holes along the sides, tiny faces in the windows. It's just the three of us in the bar, and I assume that my daddy is waiting for some regular to roll in from work. After a time, I drain the beer, call to the bartender, and ask for another. Daddy turns on me then, lips curled back from his teeth. "You don't order shit without my saying."

I nod, unsure of how to respond. I've been angling to come along with my daddy for years.

From a side door I'd not noticed before, a slender teenager slides into the room. He looks about my age, though at least a head shorter than me. Rail thin. He must go to the county school, because I've never seen him before. I nod a hello, but he's eyeing the bartender, making a beeline for him, hands jammed deep in his jean pockets.

The bartender walks over to him, and they speak in low voices. The boy pulls something from his pants, hands it to the bartender, and leaves quickly through the same door.

"That your boy?" my daddy says.

The bartender nods. He unrolls a sheaf of bills, sets them on the bar in front of us.

"Count it," my daddy says. I reach for the money, but he shakes his head. "Not you. Him."

The bartender picks up the bills, smooths them, works to shuffle them into some order. He begins counting them out onto the bar, his eyes never leaving the bills. When he's done, we all know that $167 sits before us, though I'm the only one who doesn't know if that's enough or not.

"Why?" my daddy says.

The bartender says, "Gray, I didn't mean—"

Daddy waves a hand, cutting the man off. "This is my son, Gray Junior. Looks just like his old man."

The bartender eyes me, nods, though my daddy did not phrase it as a question.

"Give Gray Junior your hand."

The man looks confused, but my daddy repeats his demand. The bartender extends his hand to me, and I take it, dry and rough between my palms.

"Hold it on the bar top there," my daddy says, digging in his pocket. I pin the man's hand to the bar, but my daddy says, "Palm up, boy." I flip the hand over, hold it firm.

Daddy takes a small metal contraption and a tiny black bottle from one pocket. There's a motor on the metal thing, a small series of gears and wiring that crowds the middle. At one end, a needle protrudes. He pushes a button. The thing hums. The needle vibrates, and my daddy pops the lid from the bottle, pours a pool of black ink on the bar top, dips the needle, and sets to work on the man's hand. I hold him firm, watching the black ink mix with his blood. As far as I know, my daddy has never been a tattoo artist. He's never been any kind of artist.

The bartender's eyes slant up to the ceiling. His jaw is set. I notice that he has a mole at the base of his nose, a small, raised circle of flesh. I feel the sudden urge to release his hand, to knock my daddy from his task, but I find myself gripping harder, letting my fingernails dig into the man's skin. I imagine ink at my nails, pushing in little crescent tattoos where I hold him.

"Gray Junior, he wants to play college ball." My daddy looks up from the tattooing. "What's your boy want to do?"

The bartender meets his eyes for a moment. "He ain't much the college type."

"Don't look much the football type either." Daddy returns to his work.

"Your boy," I say, "he go out to Lux Central?"

The bartender says he does.

"We beat their asses last year," I say, because I don't know what else to tell him. On the man's hand, the tattoo is taking shape. My daddy has written his first name—our first name—along the man's lifeline.

"Now, Ethan," my daddy says. "Next time we need to have this conversation, I want you to uncurl your fist and look to my mark. Think on it awhile and see if you can't figure a way to not bring me out here for bullshit."

Ethan grimaces. "OK," he says.

"A tattoo's an interesting thing, Gray," my daddy says. "I got mine back when I was seventeen. Why don't you tell Ethan what my tattoo says?"

I've seen my daddy's tattoo many times. It spreads across the pimpled expanse of his back, obscured in places by his mat of hair. As a boy, I traced its outline when he'd let me, sounded out the words when I was old enough. "It says, 'Make some wretched fool to pay.'"

"You know where that's from, Ethan?" My daddy has begun to write our last name, and as he speaks, he pushes down harder with the needle, drawing more blood. Ethan shakes his head. Sweat beads at his forehead. He isn't fighting back, isn't pulling his hand from us or trying to drive us from his bar. My daddy's reputation has secured Ethan to this space, has rooted his hand. I think that I could stop holding him, that he would likely keep his hand there while my daddy finished his work. "It's from a song. Townes Van Zandt. You know him?"

Ethan shakes his head again.

"Hell, Ethan. He's a damn country music legend. 'Pancho and Lefty'? No? Bet you like that Nashville bullshit. See, this is what's wrong with bars these days. Was a time you could find a decent jukebox, but I bet you've got a bunch of Garth Brooks on there."

"We ain't got a jukebox," Ethan says.

"Beside the point. My tattoo's from a song called 'Mr. Mudd and Mr. Gold.' See, these two dudes play some cards, and Mr. Gold, he's on top of the world, but Mr. Mudd, he's doing poor. But things reverse, as they tend to do."

My daddy reaches for a bar napkin, wipes the blood from his work, sets back to thickening the lines of our name.

"Now, who you figure you are, Ethan? You Mr. Gold or you Mr. Mudd?"

"Mudd," Ethan says.

My daddy laughs. "It was a trick question, Ethan. You ain't neither one. See, Mr. Gold, he was on top in the beginning, and Mr. Mudd, he was on top in the end. But you, Ethan, you ain't never been on top, and you won't ever be there. This ain't a card game, Ethan. Ain't a card game at all."

My daddy wipes the needle on a napkin and hands me the device, which I put in my pocket, careful to aim the needle away from my leg. Ethan sticks his hand under the dirty faucet, washing blood and excess ink from his skin.

"Now," my daddy says, "believe my son asked for another round a while back."

——

Daddy does not follow me when, five or six beers later, I stumble out of the bar and into the reeds at the edge of the neighboring catfish farm, looking for a place to empty my stomach. I hunch over in the humid air, the tall grasses shushing around me, smelling the stench of rotting fish. When I finish, I wipe my face with my arm, and begin to walk back to the bar. It is then that I notice the boy. He's been there the whole time, I suppose.

Throwing up helped take the haze from my drunkenness, but it is taking time to shake myself free from the dulling thud at the back of my head.

The boy whistles through his teeth, confident now that he's not in the bar with our fathers. "You look like you had a good time."

"Fuck off," I say.

"No need to get pissy."

"Sorry," I say.

"My dad all right?" he says.

"I don't know. He's still working behind the bar, so I guess he is."

"I hate him," the boy says. "Makes me come out here to pay his debts. My mom's going to shit when she realizes I took the money from her stash."

We walk back into the gravel lot. I lower Daddy's tailgate, and we sit. You can usually see the stars out here in the county, can pinpoint constellations, though the only ones I know are the dippers. Tonight, the cloud cover's so thick I can't even see them.

"You shouldn't hate your father," I say.

"He's a piece of shit."

The boy's shoulder brushes mine. "People can't help what they are," I say and think of Drew's leg, of the new angle I'd snapped it into. I think of his tears. I'd never seen him cry before that. When we were eight, I watched him ride his bike one-handed, blowing into the mouth of a glass Coke bottle to produce that hollow hum. He hit the curb unevenly, flew over the handlebars, landed hands first, still gripping the bottle. The cut it laced into his palm severed some nerve endings, has kept him from feeling anything in his ring finger ever since. I wrapped my shirt against his bleeding, and even then, he didn't cry.

This afternoon, I leaned forward, put my forehead to his, said, "I'm sorry, I'm sorry, I'm sorry."

Through gritted teeth, he said, "Shut up, Gray. Ain't your fault."

But it was my fault. Drew knew that, and I knew it too. I'd never hit someone that hard. I'd wanted it to hurt.

I feel tears at my cheeks, feel them rolling down through the stubble I'm hoping will become a beard. The boy at my side begins to laugh, says, "You crying, pussy?"

It takes no effort at all to topple him from the tailgate, to sprawl him in the dirt, to throw myself on him.

In the coming years, I will brag about the scars this boy leaves on my knuckles. I will sneer my love of them frequently in the detention center, will show them to girls in bars, will flash them at boys I want to break and later at boys I want to bed. Eventually, I will outgrow the novelty of their thick whiteness, and then I will lie about them, will tell a man I love that I worked in a wood shop as a teenager, that splinters of my trade sliced leavings into my flesh. I will begin to understand that hate and love do not have to be partnered in us.

Tonight, though, I slip the tattoo machine from my pocket. The boy makes a wet, rasping wheeze, but he's not putting up a fight anymore, and once I turn the machine on, its hum joins the oxidizers, and I can't hear the boy breathing at all anymore, even as I begin to mark him with my name.

A Guest of the Program

Here's how you do it. First, identify the recruit. In those early days, without recruiting services or a lot of tape, we did that by developing regional connections with high school coaches. Most of the time, they'd call you, say, "Look, Tommy, we've got this kid ..."

It's 1979, and they've checked in. The motel is just a little building in a gravel lot. A string of six rooms and an office. The clerk gets an extra off-the-books hundred each time they come out here. He flips on the "No Vacancy" sign while they get the kids situated in their rooms. Two per room. Twelve kids total, the crowning jewels of this year's Mississippi Tech signing class. Millinghaus and Tommy will sleep in shifts on the bus. They've been driving since morning, hitting every little corner of the state, picking up the kids from their parents' houses, loading them in, and hauling off to another town for another kid. Here, in Tupelo, they'll stay for the night. In the rooms, the kids will watch the color TVs, talk about drinking and girls and sex and football. Outside, Tommy and Millinghaus will patrol, make sure there aren't any sneak-outs, and watch for the cruising of coaches from Bama and LSU and Arkansas. In the morning, they'll load up and drive the hour to Wyeth, where these players will sign their scholarship papers. Some of them will stay, will enroll in classes at Tech right away, but most of them will be carried back to their parents, who will hug them and congratulate them on getting into college. Tommy and Millinghaus will get handshakes and will give assurances that the children will be in good hands, that at Tech the boys will be molded into good men.

Second, you've got to scout the prospect. The assessments of high school coaches are unreliable, so seeing the recruit with your own eyes is the most important part of the process. You should go out in two-coach teams. The first coach will be the lead recruiter for that area. The second coach will be the position coach the recruit will play for, should he come to your school. Get there early. Do all the requisite glad-handing, but make sure to get seated for practice. Other coaches from other programs will arrive late, will have to talk to the high school coaches and do their chit-chatting while practice begins or after it ends. You do not want to be in this group. You want to be watching your player from start to finish.

Ask yourself: Does he hustle? Is he vocal during warm-ups? Does he complain about injuries or perceived slights while on the sideline? How does he look on the hoof? Does he have the frame to add more muscle?

———

Tommy knew Room 3 would be a problem. It's eleven o'clock and Tommy's walking past when he hears the telltale clink of a bottle hitting the lip of a glass. He'd been banking on a 2:00 a.m. jailbreak, but from the sound of it, the boys got started early. He and Millinghaus checked bags and pockets for stashed bottles, but Collins must have snuck one past. Tommy unlocks the door and steps in.

Eldon Collins is on the bed, taking a swig of whiskey, and Willy Wiggins, his teammate, the one Tech really wants, is standing in the door of the bathroom, holding a full cup.

"Hand it over," Tommy says.

Collins looks at him blankly and takes another pull from the bottle. Tommy's across the room quick, snatching it from his hands. Collins tries to swipe back, but with his free hand. Tommy pushes him against the headboard of the bed. Collins is small and wiry, and Tommy's got fifty or sixty pounds on him at least. "Don't," Tommy says, but Collins pushes his arm away and is up off the bed, bowing up.

———

Once your evaluation is complete, you've got to consult with the other coaches. Weigh the pros and cons of this player as opposed to others at his position. If you were able to get any game tape from his coaches, show that to the room. Watch for flaws in mechanics. If he's a quarterback, is his motion smooth? How is his footwork? Can he throw from under center, or has he only worked out of the shotgun? If a receiver, how is his route-running? Does he go up and fight for the ball in traffic? No matter the position, you will have questions that must be answered. Ideally, the position coach who helped scout him will have some insight. He'll be able to offer comparisons to current or former players. As the lead recruiter, you should be less concerned with on-the-field performance and more focused on intangibles. Is he a leader on his high school team? Good student? Does he get in trouble with his parents or, worse yet, the police?

———

Eldon Collins shouldn't have been offered a scholarship by Mississippi Tech. Everyone knows this, including Eldon. In the film room with the other coaches, Tommy vouched for the kid. "He's fast," he said. "Still raw in his route-running, and he struggles getting separation from DBs, but there's a lot of potential there."

Millinghaus shot Tommy a look. "Let's be honest, Tom. The potential is that we'll sign Wiggins if we take Collins."

Tommy could not argue with this. Wiggins was the big fish, the player who would, Tommy was certain, be an All-American, and he was also Collins's best friend. The boys wanted to play together in college, had told Tommy this over the phone, saying that they wanted to make a mark wherever they went.

"I'm not going to say Wiggins isn't my priority," Tommy said. "We can afford to take a flier on Collins. If nothing else, we'll put him back there returning kicks. He's got straight-line speed."

Coach had been silent through most of the discussion, offering only a grunt here or there, but now he spoke up. "Character?"

"Clean slate. Passing grades, no arrests." This was technically true.

"Offer him," Coach said. "You're responsible, Tom."

So, they'd gone all in on Wiggins and, by extension, Collins. That was four months ago. Since then, there had been grade issues, there had been complaints, and there had been an arrest that Tommy got scrapped from Collins's record with a few well-placed phone calls.

Now, Collins says, "Get the fuck out of my face."

———

Contact the parents. They should always be your first step. Before you approach the prospect's coach again—or even the prospect himself—you must make contact with the parents. Show genuine concern for the player. Provide enough details to prove that you know something more about him than the average coach. Give examples of the players you've helped at your school. Shake hands firmly. Smile and thank them for the pecan pie. If you must lie, do it in such a fashion that they will not ever be able to learn the truth. In short, instill confidence. Make them see that their son can go to no better program, that he cannot be left in better care, that whatever faults he might have in his game or his character will be corrected with swiftness and compassion.

———

Wiggins comes across the room fast and wraps his arms around Collins. He pulls him back before it can escalate. "Motherfucker," Collins says. "Motherfucker." Tommy walks past them into the bathroom. It's a small room, done up in pastel green. There's a ring of brown sludge in the sink. Tommy pours the whiskey in. It gurgles going down, struggling through some blockage.

Tommy can still hear Collins chanting, "Motherfucker, motherfucker, motherfucker," and he thinks again about hitting the kid. It'd be easy to just walk across the room and smack him across the face hard enough to teach him something, but then Tommy thinks of how quickly Wiggins got across the room. He thinks of how rare that speed is for a guy his size. They need Wiggins, and Tommy needs Collins to get him. Collins will learn discipline. Tommy must teach him. He knows what to do.

Collins is sitting on the edge of the bed, Wiggins standing in front of him, arms crossed. He says, "You going to tell Coach?"

Tommy ignores the question, walks to the door. Outside, the night has turned bitterly cold. It's damp, and Tommy feels the weight of all that cold wet in his chest. He climbs onto the bus, where at least the wind is abated. Millinghaus is asleep under a bundle of jackets. His snoring rises up and fills the space. Tommy finds his bag, digs through, and then he's back out of the bus, moving across the parking lot quick, in through the door that he left unlocked, and he's grabbing Collins by the arm, hauling him out the door with Wiggins asking what's happening, what's happening, but Tommy moves forward, swinging Collins out of Wiggins's sight before he cocks the gun and holds it to Collins's face.

The boy coughs once, pops his knuckles, and looks at Tommy, who realizes that his hand is shaking, the barrel of the pistol bobbing and weaving, and he tells himself it's just the cold.

———

Accept the prospect's commitment only after confirming that the parents are alright with it. If the prospect is big-time, stay in his town as much as possible. There will be other coaches from other programs, and you'll need to fend them off. You'll need to make sure they don't get in his ear. The best way to do this is to limit his availability. Arrange for his coach to close practices. Have him hustle the prospect onto the team bus right after games. Tell the parents not to let any coaches into the living room. If you hear that a particular coach from a particular program is coming, set the prospect up at a friend's house for the night. Meet the opposing coach out front. Be courteous. Say that you don't know where the kid could have gotten to. Say that you're waiting for him too. Talk shop. When he gives up and leaves, slap him on the back, tell him if you see the prospect, you'll mention that he came by. Retrieve your prospect, take him home. Tell him and his parents that you are the only one who can be trusted.

———

"Come on," Tommy says, motioning with the gun, trying to play its wobbling off as an intended movement. Collins begins walking.

They move to the back of the motel, to the big grassy field that's overgrown with weeds. Tommy knows that ten feet deep in those weeds is an old couch. His first trip to this motel, he found a prospect on that couch, his head in the lap of some local girl. He pushes Collins through the weeds and makes him sit.

"Coach—" he starts to say, but Tommy cuts him off.

"Listen." Tommy slides the gun into his waistband. "Why'd you bring that whiskey?"

Collins shakes his head.

"Tell me," Tommy says.

"I didn't bring it."

"Don't lie." Tommy rests his hand on the gun, and for a minute, he feels like he really does have some authority.

"I didn't. Willy found it under the sink. Somebody left it there."

"You're lying."

The boy stands, and Tommy starts to grab for the gun, but Collins is on him before he can, and Tommy feels like an idiot for standing so close to the couch. They're struggling for the gun, and before Tommy knows it, the boy has it, and he's off through the weeds. Tommy charges after him, but Collins has speed, such speed, and Tommy can't catch up. He loses track of him. Tommy's chest heaves with the cold and the exertion. He stops running, just walks deeper out into the weeds.

———

The weeks before signing day will be the worst. Expect this. You should be in the prospect's back pocket. You are attached to his hip. You are his shadow. His friends are your friends. His family, your family. If he tells you he sings in the choir at church, you practice your hymns and get fitted for a robe.

Opposing coaches will try to bully and trick your prospect or his parents into flipping on signing day. The best way to prevent this is to take the prospect away the day before. Do the signing at your school. Never give them the chance. When the parents ask if they'll need to pay for lodging, tell them no, that their son is a guest of the program.

———

Tommy finds Collins at the edge of a creek. He's looking down into the slow trickle of water. "Eldon," Tommy says, and the boy turns. The gun isn't in his hands. "Look, come back to the room, and we'll talk through this."

Collins spits out into the tall grass. "Talk," he says.

"Just talk. Nothing's ruined yet."

He spits again. "I threw your gun out there." He motions to the water.

Tommy moves quickly to the boy, grabs him by the shirt and swings a fast, hard slap against his face. "You little shit."

The boy tries to bring his arms up, to force Tommy's hands away, but Tommy has a grip. He shakes the boy, swings him around, and throws him hard into the mud. "You little motherfucker. You aren't going to fuck this up."

Tommy is breathing hard. He remembers the adrenaline that used to surge through him when an opposing lineman said something about his mother. He'd knocked a Georgia guard on his ass, had made it a point to step on his wrist with the full weight of his cleats as he surged past. He'd missed the tackle because of the hesitation that move had caused, but he hadn't cared. He'd watched the slow ooze of blood coming from the guy's arm for the rest of the game and he had felt good.

He swings his boot against the boy's thigh. "Asshole," he says, and he wants to say more, wants to curse this boy as hard as he's kicking him, but more words aren't coming, and so he just swings his leg again and again.

After a time, he stops, turns from the boy curling into himself in the mud, and begins walking back to the motel.

From behind him, he hears a voice, husky and hesitant. "Tomorrow morning," Collins says, "I'll sign to play at Tech, and I'll make sure Willy signs his, too."

"OK," Tommy calls over his shoulder. "OK, Eldon. That's good."

The motel blurs into the darkness ahead of him, and Tommy slows his pace, stands still, listening to the shush of the weeds around them. It's only when he stops to listen that he can hear the boy crying.

———

A player must be moldable, must be capable of receiving instruction and of changing, but it is also true that he will always be what he is. This is the coach's paradox, and it is your greatest challenge once a prospect has signed. Have you figured this player correctly? Is he who you thought he was? Those questions must be answered, though they cannot be answered. Because the prospect you meet is not the same as the person beneath the helmet. There are no ground rules for knowing another person. There is no process by which you can know what anyone, yourself included, might be capable of doing.

Lake Charles

Trish shouldn't have tried the doorknob. Looking back on it now, I understand that her walk up the pavers, which separated house from gravel drive, onto the porch, settling her hand on the knob, and giving that little jiggle, well, that was the thing that did us in.

The house was in a small neighborhood at the southern end of the city. Only one road led in, even though there were lots of offshoot roads once we got in. They all dead-ended into the bayou, and this house, the one that Trish and I were standing at, sat behind a long, high fence at the end of a substantial gravel drive, right on the lip of the bayou.

We'd worked our way down the road that led to this driveway and this house, trying car doors without any luck. Our thought, whispered as we tucked down below the tall fence that shielded us from the street we'd just crept down, was to try the vehicles in this drive and then, if none were open, I'd try to jimmy a lock and see what we found. That's what I was doing, too, jimmying the lock, when Trish, who was supposed to be looking for the click of a light in a window inside the house, walked over to the pavers and then to the porch and then to the front door.

What could I do? Holler her name? I hissed a whisper, but in the shush of the bayou's water, I'm sure she didn't hear me. So she made it to the door uninterrupted and put her hand on the knob and gave it a jiggle.

We'd been working all the south Lake Charles neighborhoods, Trish and I. In those neighborhoods, people didn't expect their car to get broken into, not like in downtown or the Garden District, so you could pretty easily find ones left unlocked or with windows cracked. For the first few weeks, we stole stereos, but then we figured out it's hard to get several of those in a night and carry them back out, so we started looking for cash in the console, that kind of thing. You wouldn't believe how many old people leave their cell phones in their cars overnight. People who still have a landline. They don't think they need the cell in the evenings, I suppose, so they leave them sitting in cupholders or consoles, even on the dash sometimes. It's stupid even beyond the danger of someone like Trish or me coming along, of course. Hot as it is here, you're likely to fry that thing, leaving it there all night and into the morning, and I would have told them that if there had been a way for me to do it without admitting I also stole their phones and sold them to my buddy Greg, who managed his dad's pawn shop.

Anyway, we'd been working these neighborhoods, a stretch of about three square miles that spreads out north of the airport and all around the university. We didn't do it in order, because we didn't want a pattern. Two or three evenings a week, I'd pull up to Trish's house and honk my horn, she'd come jogging out, and we'd cruise around for a while until we came to a street that looked promising, one pretty far from others we worked on.

———

I met Trish when we were in high school, but she says she doesn't remember me. Can't blame her. I was quiet then. I didn't really loosen up until we got out of there. Something about those long, gray hallways with the purple gators painted everywhere and taffeta spirit signs taped up all over and the crush of other kids, all of it was too much for me, so I kept my head down and did my work as best I could and graduated on time. My dad was always on me to get more involved, and he even offered to switch me over to the Catholic school where all the rich kids go, but I told him no, it'd be the same over there probably. He didn't seem to get that, just shook his head and told me it was my decision.

———

After jiggling the handle, Trish turned from the door and slipped back down the pavers and over to me. I was squatting low alongside the car, the Slim Jim in my hand, eyes on all the windows of the house, searching for a telltale flicker of lamp or overhead light. But there was nothing. We could hear the dappling water of the bayou and in a tree across the way, the hoot of an owl. No lights came on and no sounds intruded on the evening, and so after a minute I stood and began again to work the Slim Jim down into the door, trying to catch the hidden clasp to pop the lock.

I'd gotten the Slim Jim from Greg. He offered it when I told him we were smashing windows and grabbing what we could. "Get your ass shot that way," he said, and he slipped the thin metal from under the counter, passed it over to me. "Don't want to go getting caught with that, now." I watched YouTube videos on how to use it and practiced on my own car, doing it again and again until I could catch the lock and pop it in a matter of seconds. I didn't realize until Trish and I got out with it that first night that not all car doors work the same, and so in the intervening weeks it had been a process of discovery, figuring out not just how to use the Slim Jim but also how to learn random car doors' inner workings.

I nearly had this one. The car was old, a big boat of a Cadillac, and I'd discovered that those popped easier than newer cars. Up the gravel drive a bit was a truck, and if I could get the Cadillac taken care of, I thought I'd give the truck a try, too. I still didn't know why Trish had gone to the door, but she was back alongside me now, her eyes peering into the car's windows, and so it seemed a minor hiccup in an otherwise successful night.

I had the Slim Jim nearly all the way down into the door, holding just the tip of it between forefinger and thumb, when the man came from around back of the house and told us to stop and stand up and not move, his voice soft and still.

———

I remember meeting Trish back in high school, even if she doesn't remember meeting me. We had history class together junior year. She sat off to the left, against the far wall, and I sat, as I always did, dead center of the classroom. There in the middle, you dodge the teacher's gaze. It's counterintuitive, but teachers always look to the front row for the pets or to the back to keep the rowdy kids in line or to the sides to make sure not to miss anyone, but they never look to the middle because they feel like they're only ever looking to the middle, even when they haven't at all.

So I sat in the middle, and she sat off to the left, and I looked toward her frequently. It was a crush, sure. Just a regular high school crush, the kind you get. I didn't know her then. Only knew how she looked and that she already seemed too old for the place, something other girls she sat with tried desperately to replicate. I admired that about her and admired, too, how she didn't even bother to shoot down Mike Richard's bullshit jokes. She just looked at him with cold eyes, and he'd shrink back away from her and her friends.

Mike tried to fuck with me once, tried to pick on the quiet kid, but I stomped quick on the inside of his foot, stepped fully into his space to keep him from hitting me with his big haymaker punches, and popped him a quick jab in the throat. He toppled, and people didn't seem interested in messing with me after that. They more or less ignored me, which is eventually what guys like Mike started to do with Trish. We had that in common.

———

The man held a shotgun. Big, pump-action. A hunting gun. He had it leveled at us. Trish and I stood up. We didn't raise our hands, not yet, but we did keep them at our sides, not making any sudden movements.

He was a big man, in his fifties and broad in the way that indicates a lifetime of labor that's suddenly stopped. "What the hell are y'all doing?" he said.

"Nothing," I said.

"Like hell, nothing. Get out your wallets."

I reached to my back pocket, pulled mine out. Trish said, "I don't have mine with me."

"Toss that over here, boy."

I threw it to the gravel at his feet. He kept the shotgun leveled at us as he squatted to retrieve the wallet. He was quick and graceful in his movements, and the gun's barrel never wavered. His eye shifted from us to the wallet, back to us, back to the wallet, and I thought briefly of whether we could run for it, whether we could bolt down the gravel drive. I had no doubt this man would have shot us both if we were coming into the house, but was the jiggle of the knob and finding us at his Cadillac's door enough to drive him to kill us in our escape? I rocked up on the balls of my feet, hoping that the slight movement would clue Trish that we could run at any moment.

"Best stop that, now," the man said. "Best keep those feet planted, because I tell you one thing, you think you're going to run on me, I'll fill your asses with buckshot and not think twice on it. Maybe they'll charge me with it and maybe they won't, but it won't make your asses any less buckshot, and let me tell you something, it is no goddamn fun at all to be buckshot." As he said all of this, his eyes continued to make their way over the contents of my wallet. Trish and I didn't speak. "Got me a chunk of thigh taken out by a scattergun back in the eighties out hunting with my boys. Oldest thought he was going to swing his gun up and take aim at some ducks, but he got excited and pulled the trigger mid-swing, and about half that birdshot caught me across the top of the thigh, birdshot being the smallest and delicatest of the shots from a scattergun, the kind meant to take down a whole covey of doves by driving itty bitty balls of metal into their breasts, but it is no goddamn fun to take it in the thigh, no goddamn fun at all, and I imagine buckshot feels a damn sight worse, especially since I'm liable to fire into your scrawny asses more than just the once if it keeps you from running back down my drive."

———

What happened with Trish and me was this: I spent three years fucking around in college, coming out of my shell and discovering that I could, in fact, be around people, that I wasn't, in fact, quiet and reserved. When eventually LSU asked that I not come back, I came home to Lake Charles, where I moved in with my father, whom I told daily I'd enroll in the local college and make something of myself. At night, I acquainted myself with all the local bars I'd never gotten to go in before.

I found Trish bartending at one of these, Pappy's, a dive that sat across from a strip mall with a Books-A-Million, a Market Basket, and a Little Caesars. She didn't remember me, even when I told her that we'd gone to high school together, but she poured my beers into frosty mugs, and I drank them and tipped well and kept coming back. Soon, we became friendly, and then, eventually, we started spending time together when she wasn't working. Most of the rest of the clientele at Pappy's was older, and so she'd talk and flirt with them, going through the bartending motions before cycling back around to me, where she'd pour us shots, which she took surreptitiously since she wasn't supposed to drink on the job. After, we'd go back to her apartment and watch TV and have sex and sometimes drink more and sometimes not.

It was only after all of this happened, this slow build to routine, that the idea of car burglary came to us. It was a Thursday night. Thirsty Thursday, Pappy's called it. You got a domestic beer and a shot of well liquor for $5.50. I'd been partaking of this, and Trish had joined me in a few shots when Julie came in. She was an older lady. I'd seen her before, spoken with her, possibly played a late-night game of darts with her, though I couldn't say that with any certainty. This night, she took the stool next to mine and ordered her drinks. I asked how she was, and she said fine fine fine, but then she entered into a rant about her car having been broken into the night before.

"They didn't take nothing," she said. "Just broke my window and riffled around through my glove box. They popped my trunk and went through that, too. I had a crate of baseballs that my grandson uses for batting practice back there. They took five or ten of those, but we found them about a hundred yards away. Guess they decided a handful of beat-up baseballs was more trouble than they were worth."

"Why would someone do that?" I said. "Just bizarre."

Trish, like a good bartender, said nothing, smiled and wiped down the bar.

"I don't know," Julie said. "I've been trying to figure it out all day. I get breaking in and going through the stuff, but baseballs? I don't understand it at all."

All of us there agreed that it was beyond comprehending, and I bought Julie a round and she bought me one, and then she left. Near midnight, I had a good, solid buzz going, and the bar began to clear out, it being a summer Thursday. Trish leaned against the bar in front of me, a bored look on her face, and said, "I think I know why they did it."

"Why who did what?"

"Why they took Julie's baseballs. It's a thrill thing. Whoever broke in there wasn't some hardened criminal. Probably not a teenager desperate for weed money, either. It was someone who just wanted the thrill of it. And when they came to the baseballs, they thought they'd make for a nice memento. No telling why they dropped them. Maybe something spooked them, and they ran. But I get the impulse to take the balls."

I thought about this for a while. It made a lot of sense, of course, but I tried to wrap my mind around the idea of that kind of thrill. I'd done dumb stuff just for the doing of it before, of course. Drove drunk and jumped in a pool clothed and hit on women out of my league. I'd gotten the goose bumps of excitement from those things plenty of times, but I'd never attempted something like what Trish was describing. I told her I thought I understood that impulse, too, and that a thing like that could be fun. And she agreed that it could be. And then, Saturday, her day off, we spoke of it more on her porch, drinking electric lemonades and watching the cars go in and out, in and out of her apartment complex parking lot. Monday was Big Ass Beer Night at Pappy's, and over my thirty-two-ounce mug of Coors, I asked if she was working the next day, and she said she was not, and I asked if I could pick her up around ten, and she said that I could. And our life of crime began.

———

"So there comes a time, friends," the man said, "comes a time when you got to look in the mirror and reckon with who you find yourself to be. It's a mysterious thing, but that don't mean it's got to be complicated. You can look yourself in the eye there and say, 'Yessir, I know who I am, I am a man who will do the things need doing,' and I am here to tell you that I have looked in that mirror, and I have asked myself that question, and I have found my answer. So, if you're thinking"—he flipped my wallet open and looked at my license—"of turning tail in a moment like this, you're answering your own damned question. Your name's Tawner?"

I nodded weakly.

"Strange name, strange name." I knew the question he was going to ask before he asked it, had known that someone would ask it this night, either this man or the police he would inevitably call. Still, when he finally got to it, when he finally said the words I'd been waiting to hear, it didn't make it any easier. "Billy Tawner any kin of yours?"

"He's my father."

The man grinned wide. He flipped my wallet closed and slipped it into his pocket. "The damned DA's son's out here robbing folks? You have got to be shitting me." He started to say more, stopped himself, chuckled. He didn't seem the type of man to be short of words, but in that moment, he couldn't at all think of what to say. Finally, after a time, he motioned the shotgun to Trish. "You go on and go. Me and Tawner here'll figure this out."

I expected Trish to look at me uncertainly, to hesitate, but she turned and moved quickly down the gravel drive. I looked at the man, and he looked at me, his grin still wide. "Come on inside. We'll call your daddy."

———

A word about Trish and her place in this story: she exits the page here. I would find out later exactly what she did after he dismissed her. She walked back to my car and realized that I still had the keys in my pocket. She walked out of the neighborhood through the one road in, and she walked the quarter mile to the Shell station, where she used the phone to call a friend to pick her up. She waited for me at her apartment, waited to see if I would arrive or if she'd get a call from the jail. She says now that she was not nervous during all this, that as soon as the man told her she could go, she slipped into a deep serenity.

You might think that this story is the kind where I suddenly realize that I was enamored with childish things and that my relationship with Trish was one of those childish things. It is not that kind of story. I was enamored with childish things. Trish was, too. This night was no Rubicon, though. I didn't stop drinking in bars, and Trish didn't stop either. I didn't go back to school then, and neither did Trish. We would marry eventually, and you may now be waiting for me to tell you how I cheated on her or she cheated on me, and the marriage fell apart, but this isn't that kind of story, either.

That night, Trish waited for me, calm and clear, and when all was resolved, we moved back into the routine of our lives. We married. We bought a house. We got careers. All these things did not happen because of that night, but they also didn't happen independent from it. Causality is a strange thing, is what I'm saying.

———

The man's kitchen was cluttered with the kinds of knickknacks you would expect. Lots of blue-and-white checkered wallpaper. Lots of little wooden cutouts of boys and girls in pantaloons and dresses. Big, flowered pitchers on wooden shelves with little hearts carved into them. He sat me at his kitchen table. Across from me on the wall was a corded landline. It was the kind we'd had in my house when I was a boy.

"You should just call the police," I said.

He snorted. "Don't act tough, son. You don't want me calling the police. Don't want me calling your daddy, either."

We looked at each other.

"When I was about your age, I found myself in the middle of Vietnam. Don't talk about it much, but I got you over a barrel, so I can tell you this one story, make my point. We're out on a march, moving one ville to another, and I'm talking to my buddy Steve. Now, what you got to understand about Steve is that he don't believe in anything. Don't believe in the war nor in God a'mighty nor in the chain of command. Was the kind of guy who would slip in your foxhole just to leave you a lingering fart, something to remember him by. So we're on this little trail path, moving one spot to the next, supposed to be exercising field discipline, supposed to be nice and quiet and whispery, all raised fist and whistled warning and whatnot, but Steve, he's chatting me up at a normal volume, which out there in the middle of nothing is about loud as a scream, and our lieutenant, he keeps glancing back over his shoulder at us glaring, and a lot of the other guys are, too, trying to get us to shut the fuck up, but Steve's jabbering about this or that, talking and talking, evincing a kind of lackadaisical attitude toward the day and our surroundings and the very situation of war and all of it. I'm getting a little edgy, but also I don't want to tell Steve to shut his damned mouth because he's my friend, my only real friend over there on account of I, also, was a fart-in-your-foxhole type guy, and so I don't want to tell Steve nothing because I don't want to lose the only thing I got going over there. So, I try talking back to him, but at a lower volume, hoping maybe he'll follow my lead and lower his own voice. Years later, me and my wife'd have kids, and I tried that shit with them, too. Late night and they're hollering their heads off, and you talk real soft and quiet and hope they'll ratchet down like you have. Worked about as well in the kids' bedroom as it did in Vietnam. Steve's walking along just talking, talking, talking still at the same, steady volume, and I'm going, real whispery, 'I know, man, I hear you, you're right, buddy, you are fucking-a right,' and he's not noticing at all, and we're just moving on, moving on, and we come to this trail junction, two little shit dirt roads converging, and the lieutenant stops us moving. We take up position there while he figures out whether to continue on where we've been going or take one of the other paths, and through it all, Steve is just on and on going, telling me all about this and that and the other, his hangnails and girlfriend's letters and daddy's Cadillac and all of it, and I'm whispering on back, 'I hear you, I hear you,' and everyone out there's getting more and more pissed at him but at me, too, and I'm starting to wait for one of these damned guys to go ahead and squeeze a round out in our direction, make us shut the hell up the old fashioned way, but the bullet never comes. You know what ends up happening?"

I realized that my hands were folded together in my lap, that I'd dug the nails of the one into the flesh of the other as the old man talked. "Some Vietnamese attacked you?"

He laughed. "Hell no. Lieutenant figured out which path we was taking, and we got up and moved on along and Steve kept talking until we got where we were going, and I kept whispering, and that's all that happened. I told you that story to tell you this: sometimes a thing happens and in the moment, in the damned moment, you think it's going to set something off, trigger something to happen, change something, and even when you think back on it later, you don't know how it didn't cause anything like that. Sometimes that's what happens."

He stood from the table then, plucked his keys from a pegboard behind him. "Come on."

We walked outside and he motioned me into his Cadillac. I got in on the passenger side. The car was spotless. All rich leather and polished dash. He cranked it, backed up quickly down the gravel drive and out into the neighborhood. We passed my car, still parked around the corner right where I'd left it, edged against the line where two yards met, so anyone from one house would assume I was there visiting the other.

I pulled together enough courage to say, "Where are we going?"

The old man shook his head. "Not for you to worry with," and I thought I heard in his voice the edges of something gleeful and mean. As he steered us on out of the neighborhood and back onto Sale Street I thought about opening the door, tumbling out into a roll like they do in movies, but instead I sat still, kept my eyes fixed ahead. He let the Cadillac glide fast, steering with a palm loose on the bottom of the wheel. In the parking lot of the Shell station, Trish would have been standing propped against a gas pump, her phone against her ear. But I didn't see her, and we slid on through town.

Looking out the window as we drove, it occurred to me for the first time that after a certain hour, the town died out completely. I'd always known this in a way, I suppose, and it certainly was related to how Trish and I were able to do the things we did, but now, sitting beside the old man in his big car, passing the darkened Wendy's, the emptied Albertsons parking lot, the streetlights that flashed yellow, it came to me tangibly, as an actual idea. I thought of all the people of Lake Charles, tucked into their homes, sleeping their quiet lives, and I wondered what it said about me that I was here now, with this man, on these empty streets.

Eventually, we came to Highway 14, and he put us heading south, out of town, into the flatlands where they farm for rice and crawfish, alternating years in their paddies. Years later, I met a man who owned one of those farms, and I walked with him out into the knee-deep water in my waders, and he showed me how the crawfish traps worked. The crawfish were smart enough to find their way in, looking for the scrap of chicken neck, but too dumb to find their way back out again. I'd eaten crawfish all my life, been to boils many times each spring, but I'd never understood the animals until then, never thought of them or their lives beyond the moment of dropping them in the boil.

The old man pulled the Cadillac off the highway into a small trailer park. There were a few scattered porch lights illuminated, but out here, with no streetlights, everything was shadowy.

"You're going to do me a favor," the old man said, his eyes bouncing back and forth across the trailers. He cruised slow all the way down to the end, turned around in a little grassy field, and aimed us back toward the entrance. About midway there, he stopped in front of a newish trailer, one with a freshly made porch attached to the side of it. The wood was unvarnished, fresh from the hardware store. Alongside it sat an old Ford truck.

"Go on, hop out. Under the seat of that truck, you dig around you'll find a little .22 rifle. I want you to go on and fetch that for me."

I did not question this order, just slipped from the car, leaving the door standing open. I made my way to the Ford's driver-side door and tried the handle. Locked. I realized that I'd left the Slim Jim in the Cadillac's window. I went back around, found it still dipped down in the door, pulled it free. The old man didn't look at me as I tucked it along my side and went back over to the truck. I dropped it down into the door through the window, and in that moment, I felt what a surgeon must feel when his fingers guide the blade precisely after so many years of practicing and trying. I caught the latch, flipped the lock, pulled the door open. The truck cab was cluttered with burger wrappers and empty Old Milwaukee cans. I reached below the big bench seat and felt for the gun. I came up with it barrel first, pulled it free. It was very old, any varnish on the stock long since chipped away, and though it was a small rifle, smaller than any I'd held before, I noticed its weight, the even balance of barrel and stock. I aimed it down at my side and walked back to the Cadillac. I'd not even bothered to shut the truck's door.

As I slid in beside the old man, I heard a voice holler from the trailer behind us, a bellow that did not seem to be words at all, just a resonant burble, but the old man was already driving us away, and I was already closing the door against whatever sounds the person was making.

I set the .22 across the backseat, and the man drove fast, so fast I was sure whoever was hollering would not catch us, not in that truck, and though the man was moving fast, was driving swiftly back toward town, I felt safe there in the Cadillac, lulled in its soft leather. "Who was that?" I asked. "Why'd we steal his gun?"

"That," the old man said, "was my daddy." He didn't elaborate, didn't explain why he'd take me to steal a gun from his father. He didn't tell me stories about abuse or about games that they'd play. He told me nothing, but as he drove fast back toward town, he turned to me, and in the flash and fade of the streetlights, I saw his eyes gleam with joy.

Flood, Rotunda, Ash

They say the Sabine is rising, but I've decided not to listen. Outside, there's the hollerslamscreech of families jostling their lives into over-stuffed SUVs, but in here, the AC is still cranked, and the marble I made Geoff put in when we built the house is gleaming and cool. He'd been against it. A hardwood man, through and through. He lived in New Orleans during the season, though, and so he indulged me, since he knew I'd live here without him more than with him. Alone all the time now, I have no one to argue with about the proper flooring for this empty house. I've been lying here in the rotunda since noon, since my phone buzzed with the evacuation notice. Geoff was so careful with the marble. He laid a towel on the floor and set the note on the side table before he brought the gun to his chest. Maybe someone will knock on the door. Maybe the neighbors will have that courage, to come and ask the football star's sad widow if she needs a hand. Or maybe I'll lay here and smoke another Camel and let the little pile of ash off to my left side grow. In college, my social club made us wear white gloves in public, and we could smoke only with our left hands, while seated. I've fudged the details since then. No white gloves. No chair in this rotunda. But the burning cigarette is draped between two left-hand fingers, and when I bring it to my lips, I raise my pinkie slightly, like a debutante sipping carefully from her still-brimming teacup.

The Bagman

On Sunday mornings, the bagman burns his receipts. His wife sleeps late on these days, but the bagman rises early, layers the charcoal in the smoker box, uses lighter fluid to flame it to a brilliant, chalky whiteness. In the refrigerator, the pork shoulder is in its brine. When the charcoal is ready, he adds chunks of hickory, and as they begin to smolder, as the smoke begins to puff up from the small metal chimney at the top of the smoker, the bagman takes out his wallet, removes the week's receipts, and drops them one by one into the smoker box, where they curl and blacken and fall away to ash.

The bagman knows that he could throw them in the trash, knows that no one is looking for these receipts, and since he uses cash, no one can prove much of anything anyway, but he likes the ritual of the burning, likes to see the last shred of incrimination wither and fade. There is power in this act, and power is important to the bagman, more important, maybe, than anything else.

He has the pork on the smoker by the time his wife rises. She shuffles out to hug him good morning, to smell the wood smoke that clings to his clothes and his beard, then she goes inside and begins her day—moving through the house like an eraser, making all the detritus of the weekend disappear so that they can head into the new week in an orderly fashion, then to the bathroom, where she preps and primps before being spirited to shop or visit friends or run errands— and the bagman is left alone outside. He sits in his chair and watches the smoke chug out of the short chimney. Once every hour he stands, opens the smoker's lid, and mops the pork with a sauce made of vinegar, apple juice, and spices. By the time the pork is ready, his wife will return, and she will sit while he slowly pulls the meat from the bone, and she will tell him about her day, about the silly, inconsequential things that she did with the money he gives her. Because it went low and slow for nine hours, just like his father taught him, the meat shreds easily with a fork.

"Controlling the temperature's your first priority," his father told him, many years ago. "You've got to be patient. Don't overreact to some little fluctuation." The bagman holds this in his mind each Sunday, makes sure that in the midst of everything else—Geremy and Frank and all the rest of it—he has a handle on the rate of this burning.

———

A month after his father's funeral, the bagman went to lunch with Tony, his father's best friend. Tony coaches youth sports, and at the lunch he told the bagman what his father did. In addition to the string of pawnshops that litter the northern part of the state, the bagman inherited from his father a love for the state university's football team, which sits here in his hometown. All his life, they went to games together, tailgated, drank bourbon, and cheered wildly, but his father was not a booster. Tony explained this to the bagman. A booster is a known quantity for coaches, administrators, other teams, the NCAA. A booster has a monetary affiliation with the university. A booster cannot do the things that the bagman does.

There was a time when the bagman imagined himself in a box suite at the stadium, imagined himself and his wife cheering and drinking expensive liquor and eating expensive food. He had seen those people before, the high-level donors, and he thought that he wanted what they had, the notoriety, the influence. He thought that all of this was possible, but when he sat at lunch with Tony, he began to understand that he was not one of those people.

———

There are many things about being a bagman that the bagman dislikes. The kids are flighty, their whims shifting and fluttering with no rhyme or reason. Just when you think you have a recruit locked up, just when you think he'll honor his word—the word that you've paid for—he decides he really does want to visit LSU or Alabama or Tennessee. And then there are the seven-on-seven coaches, always looking for a little bit of side cash to sway their players to your school. When the bagman meets these men, he makes it clear that the money he's handing out is one-time-only, but even he doesn't believe this. Two weeks before signing day, the coach will post something on Facebook or Twitter about his player decommitting, and the bagman will have to drive back out to some parking lot in the southern part of the city, will have to go through the whole process again.

———

The bagman has had a scare, a knuckle-charged shock of a scare that has left him wandering through his house in a daze these past few weeks. Geremy Renfroe is missing, has been missing for nearly a month now, and the bagman knows that something ineffable can be taken from him very easily now. He watches the reports on TV, reads the message boards for chatter and rumors, and when it becomes clear that Geremy's uncle, Frank, is a person of interest in the case, the bagman begins to wait for what he knows will happen next. There is some measure of power in the waiting—not in the act itself but in the knowledge that comes with it. He redirects his mind to the waiting, breathing deep, gulping lungfuls of the smoke on Sunday mornings, letting it ratchet against his chest in a painful, enlightened way.

———

When the bagman's father died in a car crash eight years ago, the inheritance of the pawnshops was smooth. There were no other children, and his father was the sole proprietor. Just a lot of paperwork, really, and then the bagman went from an underpaid store manager at one of the shops to the owner of the whole string. Besides the one here, in the city where the bagman lives, there are locations in Tupelo and West Point and Corinth and Amory.

His shop, the shop he once managed and that he still runs five days a week, sits on the southern edge of the city, halfway between dilapidated row houses and a working-class neighborhood that bleeds into the county land. He does business with both classes of people. He gives the old Black men from the city cash advances and short-term, high-interest loans. He is not licensed to do this, but none of the men complain. They have come here for years for this service, and the bagman does not extend it to anyone else. The rednecks from out in the county bring him their too-expensive HD televisions, their car stereos, their children's laptops. He writes out receipts, holds the property, and eventually, when they cannot afford to buy it back, he sells it at a profit to other rednecks. His business is done in cash, which is the way his father designed it. He does not court new business at this location, does not advertise with billboards or mailers the way his other shops in nearby towns advertise. He relies on word of mouth. He is known here, on the edge of things, and his customers recommend him to their friends, mention one another when they come in looking to make a deal. The bagman's bank account swells with money from the other locations—deposited by the men who manage those locations—but the bagman has little to do with those other shops. To do otherwise would be to court disaster. Too much of the business in *his* shop is done in the margins, and while the money he makes doing this marginal business isn't substantial, he enjoys the process of it. He likes skirting the rules and handling what must be handled to keep that skirting quiet. He likes knowing more than anyone else—his managers, his wife—can know. Having a handle on things, keeping life steady and even, is the finest form of control the bagman knows.

When business is slow at the shop, the bagman sits behind the counter and watches videos that he finds posted on Instagram and YouTube by dermatologists who have recorded the process of removing cysts, extracting blackheads, slowly bleeding clogged pores of their accumulated buildup. The bagman does not know why he watches the videos. It is not sexual, though he has not told anyone that he watches these videos, especially not his wife, who would assume some level of complicity in the action, some desire to be the popper or the poppee. The bagman is not alone in this fascination. There is a whole, vast community that enjoys these videos, people who comment on them, ask for more, discuss technique and approach. There are popper chat rooms and message boards, though he does not go to these. He does not have any interest in discussing the videos he watches, does not see this as a hobby that requires interaction with other people. It is his and his alone, a ritual that he indulges for his own sake and for his own reasons. There is no need for connection; there is only need of the act itself, the watching, and in this he takes great pleasure.

———

Geremy Renfroe was a defensive end. The bagman identified him early— saw him play on a JV team and immediately knew the boy would be good. That night, he reached out to Tony, who reached out to the coaches, who acknowledged that, yes, they were interested in Geremy and that, yes, any help that could be provided would be appreciated. He was a hometown player. The bagman's school would have the inside track in his recruitment. The next day, the bagman introduced himself to Frank.

———

The bagman's wife is cheating on him, he is certain. Has been, he thinks, for at least eight months. Finding out was an accident. She, soaking in the bathtub, asked him to retrieve her phone from her purse downstairs. He obliged, and halfway up the staircase, the phone buzzed in his palm, and he looked at the screen, saw a text message from a strange number. It took him three weeks of sneaking her phone from her purse before he figured out her passcode. It was his high school football jersey number, repeated four times, and when the phone finally opened for him, he found texts between her and her coworker. Nothing explicit. But the implications were clear to him.

That day, when the phone made itself available, his wife was in her garden, tending her spriglets of rosemary and basil, her still-green tomatoes. He felt a slow drone of fear creep into his knuckles, the same sensation that came when, as a boy, he took the snap, dropped back, and realized his receivers would all be covered. Then, he'd simply tightened his grip on the ball, tucked it, and plowed ahead for a small gain, though now he had nothing to grip but the phone, no hole to run through, no way to release the mounting tension in his joints.

After a time, he locked the phone and slid it back into her purse. When she came to him, sweaty, dirt arcing her brow, he kissed her fully, eyes closed, hands groping for some purchase at her hips.

———

In the popping clips, the doctors use a range of tools to extract the blackheads, to burst the pimples, to wiggle the cysts' off-white dirtiness from their patients' flesh. There is a metal instrument, a slender, hooked device that is pushed around the pore, looping the blackhead free of the skin. The bagman likes these videos, but they are not his favorites. There is a procedure to the cyst videos that speaks to him on some base level: a quick piercing with the needle, the rocking motion of fingers around the edge of the wound, coaxing the filth free. Sometimes what comes free is a hard lump that must jostle its way out of the wound. Other times it is a slow leak of fluid, puss that must be shed from the wound until rich, dark blood replaces the glistening whiteness. The bagman likes these videos very much. There is a release, after that initial piercing and pushing, a slow freeing, a feeling of relief that swells within him, though he doesn't understand why he should feel these things, watching strangers being cleansed.

———

Sometimes, it seems like all the kids the bagman meets have an uncle, a caring father stand-in who is only interested in what's best for his nephew.

At his first meeting with Frank Renfroe, the bagman said, "I want you to know how much we value Geremy," and Frank nodded, smiled, said that actions spoke louder than words, that he would be handling the recruitment for his nephew.

Geremy's coach knows the bagman only vaguely. He has seen him at games, knows that he is connected to Tech, knows that he is someone to studiously avoid, and so the coach presented no hurdle in dealing directly with Frank. The boy's mother, too, seemed uninterested in getting to know the bagman. And so, the bagman and Frank got to know each other very well with no interference from any other quarters.

———

The bagman's first recruit was Leonard Goston, a defensive tackle from Amory. The boy was tall and broad, and the bagman liked the easy way he smiled when he spoke of the schools recruiting him. There was a confidence there, a steady knowledge that the schools wanted him—needed him—and Goston was cocksure enough to cater to that desire. When the bagman gave his first fumbling innuendo, his first "Is there anything we can do for you or your family?" Goston had earnestly told him that his mother's car was about to give out, that she needed to be able to get to work and back.

The bagman arranged for Goston's mother to receive a pre-owned Camry—something believable, something in her price range—from a sympathetic car dealer in a neighboring town. He made sure that the Camry was fully equipped, installed the stereo himself, out back of his shop. When he delivered it to Goston, the boy shook his hand and thanked him. In the years since, only Geremy has been as polite to the bagman, and even then, it was only on that last night.

The bagman paid Goston, his mother, and his coach close to $40,000 over the course of a year. Much of that money was culled from interest on the under-the-counter loans he offered to his customers, but a chunk of it came from other bagmen, people whom the bagman never met, people who funneled the money to him through Tony. There was plausible deniability for all of them. It can't be a network, Tony said, if no one knows each other.

During that first year, the bagman worried that his wife would discover this indiscretion, but after a time, the fear left him. He handled the bills, handled the budget. There was a steady stream of reported, taxed money that flowed in from the rest of the pawnshops, and he never had to tell his wife that they'd be tightening their belts. He gave out extra loans, didn't report some sales, and just like that, he had the money he needed.

During the seventh game of his freshman season, Leonard Goston recorded his first sack—a pivotal, jawbreaker of a hit on Auburn's easily rattled quarterback—and in the stands, in his normal seat, the bagman had hooted and whistled, had clapped his hands and said, "That's my *boy*," while all around him other fans clapped and cheered and heard nothing and knew nothing. In that fine moment, the bagman knew that he would keep doing this, keep feeding this feeling, for the rest of his life.

———

His wife does not much care for football anymore. When they were younger, she'd sit and watch games with him, though the act was less about the sport and more about his presence, his enthusiasm. She cheered because he cheered, and now, all these years later, she does not watch, and she does not cheer because he *does* do those things.

He thinks that maybe he doesn't know her at all, this once-girl who floats in and out of his days in a cloud of lavender body mist. For many years the bagman did all the laundry. He enjoyed the process of it, the steady rhythm of clothes in, clothes out, of sorting and folding and arranging in drawers and closets. His wife did the cleaning—insisted upon it—but she let him handle that mundane chore, let him portion out the fabric softener, let him fluff still-warm towels into the bathroom cabinets. There came a point, though, when her anger boiled over, when his inability to follow her complex instructions became too much for her. Shirt A must be washed on delicate and not dried. Shirt B should be washed with whites even though it is pink, and it should be dried on Permanent Press. Skirt C can be neither washed nor dried. Eventually, he ceded the task to her, let her wash her own things, and now he does one small load of clothes—his clothes—each week.

———

There is a reporter assigned to the investigation for the state's biggest newspaper. Initially, the disappearance was handled by a sportswriter, but as the weeks have shuffled on, one of the writers on the crime beat has taken the reins. He charts Geremy's last movements, from the night he disappeared, again and again: home for dinner at seven, the disagreement with his uncle at the table, leaving to run an errand he wouldn't explain, and then gone, with no explanation, with no witnesses. The reporter reiterates the lack of an alibi for Frank, who left Geremy's house shortly after he did, and he discusses the dark history of recruiting handlers in the state, of men who bled every drop of money they could from their nephews, sons, grandsons. The bagman reads the articles each morning while he sits on the porch with his wife. They take their coffee together, their chairs so close that their legs brush against one another. He considers reaching out for her hand from time to time, but he doesn't do this, doesn't make this movement. Instead, he focuses on the articles he reads, on the case that is slowly emerging against Frank. It is circumstantial, yes, and the bagman doesn't think an arrest will come unless something more is discovered, but the repetition of Frank's name still troubles him, still gives him that crackle of tension in his joints.

———

The bagman does not have pimples or blackheads himself, has none of these small wounds to cleanse from his face or back in the bathroom mirror.

He's always had good skin—a gift of genetics or good diet, he is not sure which—but sometimes he wishes for a growth to form at the side of his nose, bulbous and protruding, something that he can watch in its evolution. He imagines it swelling, drawing the eyes of the people in his shop, growing larger with each day until, finally, he can stand its presence no longer, until he can use a needle to break its surface, use his fingers to ease out all the filth.

——

Geremy's recruitment was not as easy as Goston's. Once or twice a month, the bagman took a stack of cash from the safe in his office, went to a furniture store or a clothing store or an electronics store, and bought something nice for the Renfroes. He discovered early on that it was not money they wanted, that they were not interested in envelopes of cash. Regular payments would not be disbursed, and so the bagman found an alternative. Gifts. A new flat-screen TV for their living room. A new sectional that would fit nicely in Frank's apartment. A new laptop for Geremy—to help with his schoolwork, the bagman told Frank, smiling.

Newness was the key to all the purchases. Frank did not want secondhand castoffs from the bagman's shop. He wanted to be treated well, and so the bagman treated him well. He pretended at being frustrated by this when he spoke with Tony, but the bagman secretly enjoyed this. He liked feeling the cash bulging against the confines of his wallet, liked the eyes of the clerks who rang up his purchases when he peeled off crisp hundred-dollar bills, liked, of course, holding the receipts until Sunday so that they could be burned down to ash.

——

His wife always showers when she gets home, always sluices off what she says is sweat from her time at the gym, but the bagman understands that it is more than that. The bagman sits downstairs and listens to the water pattering on the tile. Knowing that he could stand, walk upstairs, let himself into their bathroom, sit on the closed toilet, say, "I know about Hayden," is enough for him. Holding this card, clutching it tight, is enough to level off the jealousy and anger, enough to give him back what he felt slipping from him when he saw that first text message, and he can wait a while longer to bring an end to things.

——

The night Geremy disappeared, the bagman's burner cell rang. His wife was out, gone to the place she'd rather be, and the bagman, sitting on his porch drinking a beer, answered on the first ring.

"I need to talk to you about something," Geremy said.

"Where's Frank?" the bagman asked. "He doesn't like me talking to you directly."

"My uncle doesn't ... I just need to talk to you," the boy said, and the bagman agreed, named a parking lot in an abandoned strip mall. He finished his beer before he left the house.

———

For many years the bagman marinated his pork instead of brining it. The marinade had been his father's recipe, one that called for many of the same ingredients that the bagman still uses for his mopping sauce. The old man believed his marinade could seep into the meat, could tenderize it and prepare it for the slow crusting of that low, steady heat. The bagman does not use this recipe any longer, though he couldn't tell you why. The first time he brined his meat—a straight brine, just pickling salt and water—he feared that this would be a tipping point for him, the end of his progression away from his father, but when the meat took on the smoke and the dry rub flavoring, when he discovered it glistening with melted fat as he pulled it, he knew that he'd been right to veer off in this way.

———

There were tears in Geremy's eyes when he told the bagman that he wanted to go to LSU. The bagman was leaning against his truck, his arm draped over the side, into the bed. He does not know why he chose to bring the truck to this meeting instead of the car, the nice German car he spent quite a lot of money on, which he likes to show off. He chose the truck. And he stood, listening to the boy, his arm draped into the bed of the truck, his fingers grazing the tire iron absentmindedly while the boy spoke.

"I don't want you to be mad at me," the boy said.

"My uncle doesn't like it, but I got to do what's right for me," the boy said.

"I appreciate all you done for us," the boy said.

"I'll pay you back for everything when I make the league," the boy said.

———

There is a freshman from a high school in Tupelo. He is a receiver, a tall, lanky boy who still has baby-fat cheeks. When he goes up for a jump ball, the bagman can see him in his team's uniform, can see him hauling those passes down from an All-American quarterback purchased from some other city by some other bagman. He knows that he cannot create the entire team, that he does not possess that amount of power or influence or reach, but he can do his part. The receiver's father is a janitor, his mother a dollar-store manager. The bagman can feel the itch of discovery gnawing at him, the desire to know the best approach to these people, and he knows that soon he will reach out—not yet, it is still too early—and that once he reaches out, he will finesse a strategy from them. Maybe he will deliver cash or maybe he will provide new vehicles. Maybe he will give them some benefit he hasn't even come up with yet. The possibilities thrill him. And he knows, of course, that the boy might say no to his team, that he might decide to go to Auburn or Georgia or LSU. The bagman will not slip again. It was so easy with Geremy. The boy, crying earnestly. When the bagman reached down and took hold of the tire iron, he felt control slip from him. It is not a mistake he will make again, he tells himself.

In the slow bleed of his life, the bagman knows that his time might still come, that the things he has done might well lead him to ruin. He knows that one day he might confront his wife, or that maybe she will see the popping videos. The different possibilities don't matter, because the result will be the same, he knows: she will leave him for Hayden, and he will be alone. These things could come to pass.

And then there might one day be a knock at the door, and the bagman will be led away from this life and into another. If that day comes, the bagman knows that he will be able to fight off tears, that he will be able to control himself. When he permits himself to think about it, he wonders sometimes why Frank hasn't already spoken his name. He marvels at the thought that perhaps, to Frank, he is of such little consequence that he's not even worth mentioning.

They'll not find Geremy, the bagman is certain. He is buried by a dry creek bed in a deep part of the woods that sprawl out from the edge of the city, that bracket it from the suburbs. Many times, the bagman thinks of himself as belonging in these woods, the wild, harried margin between places.

They will not find Geremy, and after a time, the story will go away. The reporter and the police and everyone else will look at Frank, will think that *this man* got away with something, *this man* is lucky to have gotten out from underneath his crime. But the bagman knows that luck and fate are not real. He knows that the only lives we can live are those we carve out for ourselves. The story will fade, and the bagman will forget that any of this ever even happened, will focus instead on this young man, this receiver, who will be such a fine addition to his team. All of this will come to pass, and in the meantime, the bagman will wait and will be happy in the waiting.

The Coach's Daughter

August came full-throated that year. A shambling, sweaty hulk of a month, its air danced with lovebugs, their coupling bodies floating through open doors, cracked car windows, mouths left agape for a second too long. Reach out, crush their bodies against yours, but as soon as that pair is wiped on pant leg or tissue, another set floats past your vision. This was always the way of it in Louisiana, but that year was worse. The heat left us slick and sticky, and though my father had just paid for a new coil, by mid-afternoon each day our air conditioner stopped fighting the encroaching heat and our home began to perspire, the walls moist, the windows sheathed with beading sweat, the large slate tiles of the kitchen and hallway a slipping hazard. This inability to hold off a force larger than himself angered my father, though that summer of my thirteenth year, many things had this effect on him.

Perhaps not coincidentally, that summer also marked the start of my father's turn toward aggressive ambition. We'd moved to Bell Lake twelve years before when he accepted the head coaching job at the high school. I was only six months old, and if my father was to be believed, I lay on the bench seat of the U-Haul between my parents, crying right until the wheels touched Bell Lake asphalt. Then I stopped, knowing that we were home. He told me this story many times, always keeping a level voice, which seemed odd. Speak those words aloud and you should emphasize that closing phrase. *We were home.* That was my father, though, always willing to tell a good story, never able to tell it well.

At the high school, he coached his teams to pass only as much as they ran. On defense, they never blitzed, just played a safe high-zone. That strategy earned him winning seasons year in and year out, though his teams tended to flounder in the playoffs when safe strategy collided with superior talent. Had Bell Lake's team not been so abysmal when he arrived, he'd have been fired for never making the team a true powerhouse, but there was no pressure from the boosters. They were happy to see a winning product on the field, even if those wins were low-scoring and interspersed with close losses. His teams didn't win big, but they didn't lose big either, and that was good enough.

That summer, something changed in his mentality. He stopped looking for the stable route and began to explore something more reckless. There was no debate between me and my mother about the origins of this aggression. We spoke of it in whispers, not wanting him to hear our conversations, not wanting him to turn that hardline jaw and blank stare toward us.

My father had a veteran team, all seniors. He'd made the playoffs the year before, and while his team—in its usual fashion—had not made a deep run, there was budding optimism. There was possibility.

That summer, my mother worked days as a file clerk at a law office, and with my father incessantly watching film on that year's slate of opponents, I was left to fill my days as I pleased. During earlier summers, I'd helped my father with his preparations for the season, scouting opposing teams. He'd taught me the fundamentals of the game at an early age, and as soon as he figured out that I had a talent for organization, he started setting me up with a legal pad and game film whenever he could. That spring, he'd even enlisted my help in splicing together highlight reels to send out to college coaches and online recruiting services for some of his best players. I picked the plays, focusing mostly on touchdowns, interceptions, and sacks, since those would catch the eye of potential recruiters. Interspersed between the highlights, I included short clips of my father and the assistant coaches talking about their players' work ethic, their will to win, their heart. Everyone agreed that the videos were a success, and I'd anticipated a summer full of preparation for the upcoming season, but once my father's newfound motivation came about, he'd not asked me to help at all.

After the first weeks of summer came and went without any requests for assistance, I broached the subject with him, asking why he didn't want me watching film any longer.

We were standing in the backyard, my father swinging an old Louisville Slugger into a truck tire that lay in the dirt. It was a workout he'd used for years with his team, though he'd only recently begun doing it himself. That summer, he spent hours thudding bat to rubber, an exercise that would, he claimed, strengthen his forearms and his core.

He wiped at the sweat on his forehead with the back of his hand, took a long sip from his water bottle. "You're getting older. Need to have a life outside of my team."

"I don't mind." I hesitated for a moment. Then in a rush, before I could back down, I said, "Did I not do a good enough job last year?"

"I don't want you doing that anymore. It isn't right for you to be working for me like that."

"I've been helping every summer since I was eight."

"Things change, kiddo." Those words should have felt comforting, the words of a father gently speaking the truths of the world to his daughter, but there was a brutal finality to his tone that he'd never used with me before.

I told him that I understood, and in a way, I did, though I'd not be able to articulate what was changing or how for many years.

I turned from him then and walked into the cool house, feeling myself shift second to second, the swirling details of my life coalescing and scattering, re-forming like a swarm of bees, aligning for an attack.

———

That night I asked my mother to intervene. For weeks she had been waging a silent war against the change in my father's demeanor. She quit fixing dinner for us, started coming home from work later, spent the hours when she was home on the phone with her sister in Alabama. It was clear she was trying to get my father's attention, but as far as I could tell, her efforts were fruitless. There had always been the bruises, had always been the shadowy reminders of whatever silent fights they had in their room at night, and while those bruises became more frequent and more pronounced that summer, the conflict between them was still hidden from me. I thought, perhaps, that my father's new indifference to me might shove this conflict to the side, that if she simply spoke with him about my desire to help, she'd stop her quiet nudges and he'd stop whatever he did to her when I was not around.

Through the years, I've wondered how things might have changed if she had agreed to my request. It could very well have played out exactly as I'd hoped. My request, filtered through her, might have alleviated the strain, released the mounting pressure on their marriage. More likely, I've decided, it would have set us on a new timetable, would have escalated things. I couldn't have known that then, of course. Hindsight is as meaningless as luck, and when I made my request, those forces—luck and hindsight—were not given over to me.

My mother said no. She told me that she did not want to upset my father. She reached out and let her fingertips graze my elbow as she told me that I should work to keep him happy as well.

———

And so, for the first time in my young life, I found myself completely free for the summer. My response to this freedom—typical, I suppose, for a bookish kid—was to hole up in my room reading. I'd rise each morning and take my bike the four blocks to the public library. Bell Lake sits just to the west of the

Acadiana bayou country, at the edge of the flat land that thirty miles away will become Texas, and so biking here is easy but for the heat. I'd pedal fast on those flat streets, working up a sheen of sweat, letting the cold blast of the library's AC hit me as I went inside. I was quick about my work there, returning a stack of books I'd devoured, getting a new stack, slinging them into my backpack, and, before the first gloss of sweat had even had an opportunity to dry, hopping back on my bike and pedaling home. There, I retreated to my room, to the big box fan in the window and the slant of sunlight that filtered through my half-raised blinds. I propped my back against the fan, let it hum against me as I read. This never exactly cooled me. The pulsing churn of air lulled me, though, let me sink out of my world and into whatever book I was reading at that moment.

That summer I'd begun to read real novels for the first time. It had started with a Dean Koontz horror novel—government-made monsters, heroic animals—and that had eventually filtered to thrillers, and finally, by August, I was fully immersed in detective fiction. I'd worked through half of Lawrence Block's Matt Scudder novels, had read all of Chandler and Hammett, and had finally settled on John D. MacDonald's Travis McGee series. McGee, the rambling, ambling, shabby-boned knight errant, seemed like the end point for my summer. McGee took it easy, sipped his gin, bounced beach girls aboard his houseboat, the *Busted Flush*. I read those books and felt the thrum of the fan at my back, felt the undulating softness of that warm, moist air, and I began to believe the words my father had spoken. Something was changing within me as well.

————

The day I met Jason, I rode out from the library a little after nine, intending to go home, intending to take up my spot against the fan. The bike was a ten-speed, one that I'd taught myself to ride, having only ever been on fixed-gear Huffys handed down from my cousins, brought back from family vacations to Alabama in the bed of my father's truck. I'd found the ten-speed in a thrift shop that spring, had bought it with my allowance money and spent hours learning to shift gears, my knees, elbows, and palms bloodied from my failings.

As I moved out from the library that day, taking the bike into the street, a gust of cool wind hit me, braced me with shock at its unexpected presence. Without giving it much thought, I turned from my path home and rode into the wind, moving across town until I finally reached the lakeshore. There, on the makeshift beach—dirty, brown sand littered with the detritus of out-of-town rednecks—I took up a spot on the slope heading down to the water.

The beach was mostly deserted, and other than a cluster of boys off in the distance near the edge of the water, I was alone. I took a book from my backpack, lay back against the sand, and began to read, though I found myself glancing to the boys after each paragraph and, eventually, after each sentence. There were five of them, and they were all in my grade at Bell Lake Middle, though I'd never had much to do with them. I was in advanced classes, straight-lining toward college prep coursework in high school, and they were in all the basics. Still, the school wasn't large, and I recognized them, even if we'd never spoken. They were playing at fishing, casting their lines, reeling in, recasting, laughing and punching and rollicking the way they did when I passed them in the halls of our school.

Finally, I dropped my book, watching them without pretense. In my back, I felt a tingling vibration, like the hum of the fan, like the burn that lingers after you knock your funny bone. It traveled slowly from the base of my spine up to my neck, a feeling of pain and pleasure and fear for the harm that can be done when the right nerve is jangled. Before I could stop myself, before I knew what had overtaken me, I hollered, "You won't catch anything like that."

They turned, startled. One boy—Jason, a pretty decent receiver on the middle school team—called back, "We ain't trying to catch anything."

I rose from the sand, dropped the book, and made my way down the slope to them. "What are you doing if you're not trying to catch fish?"

Jason smiled, winked at me. He dropped his pole, made a pretend reeling motion in my direction and said, "Trying to catch pretty girls."

They all laughed at this, but I just blushed, mumbled something about needing to get home. I took to my bike then, not even remembering to grab my book. Months later, I'd pay the library nearly forty dollars from my allowance, penance for never returning that novel, though by the time that happened, this seemed like a small price to pay for some retribution.

———

That was the night I finally saw my father hit my mother. I'd spent the afternoon back in my room reading, trying not to think about the beach, trying not to think about Jason, but as I moved through the pages of a new novel, I kept thinking of the playful half-smile Jason had shot my way. When my mother called me down for dinner—a surprise in and of itself—I'd formulated a plan.

My father was already seated at the table, waiting for his meal, the first my mother had cooked all week. They must have fought about it, because she went all in, frying pork chops, simmering field peas, roasting squash and zucchini from her garden. As she brought the food out, I said, "Daddy, you're going to have a pretty good receiver next year."

He'd been sitting with his hands folded in front of him, his eyes tracking my mother as she went in and out of the kitchen, but when I spoke he dropped his hands to his lap and shifted his gaze to me. "Who's that, sweetie?"

"A friend of mine," I said. "He's in my grade, and he's my friend. His name's Jason."

My father drummed his fingers, nearly all of them, on the tabletop. This was a habit of his, one I'd seen many times before while sitting beside him watching film. The only finger that didn't strike hard against the surface was the pinkie finger on his right hand, which jutted up and out. That finger never straightened fully, but he couldn't curl it either. In his playing days, a defensive back had planted his shoulder against my father's hand, and the pinkie had shattered. My father refused medical treatment for the duration of the season, and when all was said and done, the finger never fully healed because of it. My father never balled that fist, never used that hand to lift things, if he could avoid it. He knew that these actions brought attention to the angled finger, to what he thought of as the fracturing of his career as a player, and so he masked it as best he could.

"Bring him on over one day," my father said. "We'll have him some dinner ready. Right, Susan?" My father shot a glance at my mother, who was still ferrying food to the table. "Could have us some dinner on time if we had company, hey?"

My mother said nothing, simply set down the bowl of field peas with a gentle *click*. In the years since, I've wondered about that motion, wondered if it was the delicacy of the placement that caused it. If she'd slammed the bowl down, shattered it on the surface, would my father have still launched from his seat, pulled his right hand back, and swung? Would she have still crumpled to the floor crying while he stared at her, breathing bull-hard? Would I have still stood slowly, still slipped carefully into the hall? Would I have gone red-faced at the surging adrenaline, felt the sharp tingle of selfish possibility, reached a hand to the side of my head, tangling my fingers into the hair until I could pull a hard fistful, driving myself to tears that would not be heard?

My mother was composed when she brought the plate to my room. It was an overloaded apology of food, pork chops and squash and zucchini and peas puddling into one another. I was sitting against the fan, letting my eyes move across words, letting my fingers turn pages, though the meaning of what I read passed before my vision like the blurred shifting of bees swarming before their attack.

I closed my book, said nothing to her.

"I brought you some dinner." She set the plate on the corner of my desk. "You can come eat with us if you want." She glanced over her shoulder, and as she did, the sharp, dark bruise turned full to me. "Or you can eat in here."

I looked at her for a long time before opening my book and returning my eyes to it, and though she left the room the same way she'd entered—closing the door with another soft, gentle, constrained *click*—I felt something acidic welling in my stomach, something inexplicable, governed by a force I could not then and still do not understand, though I have spent these intervening years trying as best I can.

———

Jason and his friends were fishing again. I didn't hesitate this time, just walked down to join them at the edge of the lake. They nodded their hellos, though Jason's eyes lingered on mine, holding contact for a beat longer than was comfortable. My presence was all the invitation they needed to begin showing off. They knocked one another around for a while, punching and grinning through middle school jokes, searching for my approval, I think.

This was new territory for me. When I'd moved into sixth grade two years earlier, the transition from elementary to middle school had been difficult. In the new social stratus, in a world where there was a five-minute window every hour for interacting in the hallways, I found myself unable to keep up with my old friends, who took to the flirting and gossiping with a zeal I couldn't mimic. I retreated into my classes. With very little effort, I directed my crushes and attractions to faculty members, to the thirty-something biology teacher whose stubble of beard was still well out of reach for my male peers.

As the boys joked with one another, I reached down and picked up Jason's pole and cast his line into the water. Though they continued their joking play, I let my line sit with only the occasional yank to move my bait around.

The boys were more surprised than I was when my line bobbed, and I pulled in a large catfish. As I reeled the line in, Jason and the others jumped back, out of the way of the spiny fins.

"Let it down there on the ground," Jason said. "We'll clean it once it's dead."

I set the fish down and walked to the little tackle box they'd brought with them. They didn't have much in the way of gear—nothing like my father's big, six-tray kit—but there were kitchen shears and a dull-looking fillet knife. I tested the knife's blade and decided that, despite its dullness, it was flexible enough to work.

I pinned the fish's tail with my tennis shoe and held its head firm on the ground to keep it from whipping around on me. Using the shears, I snipped the dorsal and pectoral fins. I dropped to my haunches, picked up the wriggling fish, and spread it on the flat lid of the tackle box.

"We usually just let them die," Jason said, though there was no urgency in his voice. "Ain't you supposed to skin it first?"

"Not if you fillet them alive," I said, sliding the knife in at the angle I'd practiced with my father, letting the knife do the work. I moved the blade carefully, shifting directions as I separated the meat from the body. "Main thing," I said, "is to make sure you don't rupture the organs. That changes the whole taste of the fish, makes it more muddy. A catfish isn't like any other fish. With crappie or bream, you can puncture something, and it's just messy for cleanup, but the meat still tastes fine. Catfish are dirtier, though, and because of that, there's a higher chance that you'll ruin the meat if you let any of that junk leak out."

I raised a fillet—a bit ragged from the weak blade but whole. I used the knife to strip the skin from it and tossed the meat to one of the other boys before flipping the fish over and repeating the process on the other side. When I was done, I punctured the air bladder and threw the remains in the water.

"Where'd you learn to do all that?" Jason said.

"My dad. We go fishing on my uncle's land in Alabama. He's got eight or nine acres out past Gordo. He's got a bunch of bees, farms their honey, but I told him they're a waste of time. Colonies are dying off at a crazy high rate, and he won't make his money back in the long run."

One of the boys said, "Who gives a shit?" but Jason swung on him, gave him a hard thump on his upper arm.

"We need them for pollination," I said, though I bit back a longer explanation.

"Forget that," Jason said. "Will you tell us what Coach is like? We're going to try out for the team next year."

I hadn't thought that Jason recognized me. For the last two days, I'd been running on pure adrenaline, the thrum in my back pushing me forward without allowing me time to overanalyze what I was doing. Now, that feeling had worn off, and I wanted to know if Jason was only being nice to me because of my father. I didn't ask him, though. I turned from the boys, not wanting them to see the tears welling in my eyes, and for the second time, I pedaled away, going hard over the cracked sidewalk, nearly losing my balance as my wheels bounced and skidded over protruding tree limbs, and though I felt the burning of embarrassment, I felt something else, too, a pulsing vibrancy that nagged at my head, that told me that ambition might not be as bad a thing as my mother seemed to think.

My mother and I didn't speak of the incident, but moving forward, meals were elaborate and on time. She sat quietly while we ate the food she'd prepared. Her response to his violence was to move inward, and she did this completely. She didn't ask me about school, didn't ask him about his days either. She studied her peas, ate a quarter of the food on her plate, cleaned our mess, quietly stacked the dishes for washing. When I'd tell her goodnight before moving to my room, she pecked my cheek, but even in that gesture of affection, I felt the distance between us, between who we had been and who we were becoming. In my room at night, I read my books propped against the fan. In my head, the word *Jason Jason Jason Jason Jason Jason* repeated unbidden, thrumming in time to the fan until all the rest of it faded, and I could feel the warm comfort of the unknown.

The first day of eighth grade was much the same as the first day of seventh grade. I moved through the halls with my backpack hoisted high, my head down. If I passed Jason between classes, I didn't allow myself to know it. Though there was a part of me pushing to connect in a way that I didn't understand, I made myself revert to what I'd spent the previous years becoming. I went to my classes, did my work, ate my lunch alone in a corner of the cafeteria.

Once fall practice started, we saw less of my father, but this didn't stop my mother from continuing to prepare the meals my father had demanded. She cooked the meals to his specifications, kept them warm for when he finally came home—nine or ten o'clock each night. One evening, I watched him sidle up to her, lace his fingers around her wrist while he kissed her neck. When he released her wrist, the imprint of his large hand remained, white streaks of pressure from four fingers, the only missing mark that of his ruined pinkie.

Jason wore his school uniform, a green polo tucked into khaki pants. He was waiting for me beside our mailbox, his arm casually draped over it. His limbs were lanky, his features angular, and there was an ease to the way he leaned. I wondered how he made himself that fluid. There was always a jangling edge to *my* motions, but when he saw me, Jason unfolded himself to full height in a smooth movement. His easy grin spread out, and he said, "Hey."

"Hi," I said.

"Waved at you in the hall today."

"I'm sorry. I guess I didn't see you."

"No worries."

I stood a few feet from him, unsure of what to say next. He leveled his gray eyes on me, let them swing down my body in a way that both made me uncomfortable and giddy.

"What are you doing this afternoon?" he asked.

"Homework."

"Want to hang out instead?"

My gut told me to turn from him, to walk into my house without another word, to retreat the way that I had each of the times I'd talked with him before, but there was something different about him being here with me in front of my home. I reached out and took his hand, warm and moist. In the humid afternoon, I couldn't tell if that sweat was from the weather or his nervousness, and in the moment, I didn't care. I led him to the backyard.

———

We were sitting together on the old tire, sharing Jason's earbuds and listening to music I didn't recognize, when my father walked into the backyard.

"Who are you?" my father said.

I stood. "This is Jason. He's the receiver I was telling—"

"Go inside," my father said. He closed the distance between us before I could respond. His four-finger grip on my shoulder burned.

I walked to the back door, the thundering of blood in my ears blocking out my father's loud voice, blocking the precise nature of what he said to Jason about *his* home, *his* daughter.

———

He came to my room after. I was leaned against the fan, though I hadn't turned it on. He stood in my doorway a long time, looking me over.

"What were you doing with him?"

"We were listening to music."

"I know . . ." he began, but he trailed off. He shook his head, reached up and held the top of the doorframe, twisted at the waist until his lower back crackled.

"We were just listening to music," I said.

"That's what you said."

"He's my friend."

He walked slowly across the room, closed his hand around my wrist, his fingers grinding skin and bone. "You were born sick," he said. "Just like your mother."

I closed my eyes against the pain, thought of the pulse of the fan, the scattered formation of my uncle's bees. After a time, his grip slackened, and he left my room.

———

Seated together at our dinner table, my mother's eyes settled on my wrist. With an unbidden, theatrical flourish, I aimed the bruise at her, willed her to see it, to understand what was happening.

One summer while visiting my uncle, I walked with him to his hives, and while he talked absently about them, I reached a bare hand out to the swarm, let them cover my skin. My uncle told me to keep very still, and for a time I did, but then, with precision, I curled my hand into a fist and felt the stinging begin.

At the dinner table, my father did not seem to notice my mother's expression or the brazen cant of my darkened wrist.

———

My father was asleep in his recliner when I went to bed. I sat against the humming fan. I did not read, and I did not sleep. It was very late when I heard the gentle *click* of the back door. I turned and looked out the window. My mother walked out to the old tire and picked up the Louisville Slugger. She hefted its weight, tested the swing. She'd played softball in college. That's how they'd met. My father the football player, my mother the catcher. When I'd played as a child, she taught me the correct pivot, how to redistribute my weight in the correct fashion as I brought the bat through the air.

As she came inside, I moved into the upstairs hallway, positioned myself at the top of the stairs. I heard a dull, metallic *thunk*. Was she tapping the bat against the refrigerator? The countertop? I do not know, though in the years since, I've tried to consider the timbre of that *thunk*, have tried to reason my way to the correct answer.

I do know that as she left the kitchen and moved to the hallway, she dropped the tip of the bat to the tile floor. As she walked, a slow grinding of metal against slate filled the silence of the house. First, the grind of bat on tile, then a soft *click* of the tip dropping to the grout between the tiles. Grind. *Click*. Grind. *Click*. I sat on the top step and closed my eyes. I remember now the feel of the wooden stair beneath my fingers, the hinting grooves of its grain, polished over many years by my mother so that it was only barely perceptible.

Downstairs, my mother must have thought I was asleep.

When I opened my eyes, my mother was below me in the hallway. She was letting the end of the bat tap the glass of our framed family pictures. She moved along the line, letting the bat settle against each one. Finally, she turned to the living room, dropped the bat to the floor again. Grind. *Click*.

From my vantage point, I could see only the back of the recliner, a faint outline of my father's balding head. He was tipped back. His mouth must have been slack in a silent snore. As my mother moved out of view, she lifted the bat, and I wondered if this was what the bees felt before they stung. I had shown her my wrist, had made her look at the harm that had been done, and now, though she held the bat, this attack would be mine, the sinking of my stinger in flesh, the separation of violence from my body. I would leave my stinger in him, and I would bleed out here from the wound I'd given to myself.

The bat's arc was fast and sudden, and surely my father did not see it coming.

In the Cold River

At the end, Ellen's freckles disappeared. They'd smattered the bridge of her nose for as long as I'd known her, a period that spanned childhood, teenage years, and nearly ten years of marriage as adults. When we'd first dated as high schoolers, I'd kiss the freckles as we made love. It made her giggle then, which made her clench. A game, you see. The last weeks, they simply vanished, leaving behind only smooth, yellow-gray skin. Of the things I remember from after is this: me, drunk or nearly drunk or just recovering from being drunk, asking the funeral home proprietor if I could see her to check if they'd come back. He advised against it, gently offered to have their man paint some new ones on. It was one of the things I'd meant to ask a doctor about, though I never did.

———

The children are talking about monsters. We've built the bonfire high, and they sit too close, even with the cold. We, the adults and the older siblings and a neighbor or two, are near drunk, and the children know this, but they have their games, and they stick to them, even when we get this way.

Mary Ellis, my daughter, says, "My monster has tree branches for teeth and a crocodile tongue." She draws the words out slowly, doing her six-year-old best to scare her friends. "His fingers are lions, and his hair is poison."

I stand from my camp chair, toe the edge of a log, nudge it deeper into the fire. Sparks scatter in the air, and Mary Ellis and her friends swing their flashlights to the embers, a game they've been playing all evening. "I got that one!" someone shrieks, the beams silky in the smoke. They track the embers until they wink out.

"What about his feet?" I ask.

"Forks."

"His feet are made of forks?"

Before Mary Ellis can answer, I feel a hand minnow into my back pocket. It's Sandra, the only other single parent in this group. We have been sleeping together for two months, but no one knows this, and a hand in my pocket is the kind of acknowledgment we've both agreed to avoid. All night we've been catching eyes from across the clearing, and I think she, too, has been trying to figure a way for us to sneak off to one of our vehicles without the children or the other parents or the siblings or the one or two neighbors discovering.

I turn to Sandra, and she slips her hand from my pocket. "What kind of forks?" she asks Mary Ellis.

My daughter looks at the two of us, standing above her and her friends. "Not little forks," she says. She tucks her flashlight beneath her chin. "Big forks. The fork you stab the turkey with when you're cutting it. Every toe is one of those forks."

"He doesn't trip over those?" Sandra says.

Mary Ellis's look turns serious. "He's a monster. He doesn't trip at all. He eats children and people and kind animals."

At the cooler, I nudge Hébert to one side. He's been sitting here, policing the beer, making sure that the older siblings don't get too drunk. I shuffle a can of High Life from the ice. "Sip of bourbon?" Hébert asks, tipping an open bottle in my direction. I take it. Two years ago, when Sandra was still married to Calvin, when my wife Ellen was still alive, Hébert and Sandra fucked five or six times. Sandra disclosed this at the start, told me that it had been a couple of months' worth of meetings, that it had played a part in her split from Calvin, though he'd been unfaithful as well. She told me that Hébert's wife, Lucille, did not know and that she and Hébert would prefer to keep it that way, as Lucille and Sandra were best friends, had been best friends for nearly twenty years. I have kept this secret, though I wonder if Hébert knows about us. I pass the bottle back.

———

We kept the diagnosis from Mary Ellis, kept it from her when the two of us cried ragged in our bedroom every night and every morning while she watched Netflix and read books, kept it from her when Ellen began losing appetite and weight, kept it from her when Ellen's eyes went glassy and she had a hard time holding concentration. We didn't tell Mary Ellis what was happening until near the end, though looking back on it now, the end came so rapidly our withholding didn't last that long.

Ellen held her hand and offered her all the medical terminology and then offered the explanations that accompanied them. It was a strange pantomime of the conversations we'd had with the specialists for months. There was a logic to Mary Ellis's response. That's not to suggest that she didn't get upset, that she didn't rage against her mother's illness. She did. But her reactions were so visceral and immediate—the tears, the questions—that they made a kind of perfect sense, felt so natural and normal, especially when I compare them to the ways Ellen and I responded to the same news.

After, we went for ice cream, and the three of us sat with our different flavors, licked the melt.

———

Sandra takes my hand and leads me out into the woods, away from the clearing. This land belongs to Hébert's family. Fifty acres out in the wilds of central Louisiana. They used to hunt on it, but Hébert has sworn off the practice. He claims this is not because of any change in philosophy regarding animal cruelty or gun rights or anything else, but he won't provide any other reasoning beyond saying that he never much liked deer sausage anyway.

As we move into the dark, I bring Sandra's hand to my lips, kiss her knuckles. She stops, and we sit together on the blanket of pine straw. As we fuss one another out of our clothes, the needles dig into our skin, but it doesn't slow us. I have never minded a brittle sting. In the distance, we hear the whoop and laugh of one of the kids, and for a moment, I let myself think that being whole is still possible.

———

It was a month before the end when Ellen and I had the talk. Since the diagnosis, I'd expected her to push me with some kind of "I want you to move on once I'm gone, don't let Mary Ellis grow up without a mother" patter. We were in the car. We'd left an appointment. Mary Ellis was in school. It was just the two of us. We'd driven in silence for a while, but Ellen asked me to pull over. I thought she might have to vomit, and so when I pulled into a Taco Bell, I reached for the glove compartment, meaning to get napkins out to help her clean up after. She touched my hand, pushed it gently back to the wheel.

"You are going to do what you're going to do," she said. She looked out the window at the lunchtime drive-thru line. "When I'm gone, I mean. You're going to do what you want or need, and I understand that."

"Ellen," I said, "we don't have to—"

"Shut up. There's so much that I'm not given anymore. Being selfish is the one thing I can hold onto, so I want you to understand something. When I'm gone, when you're doing what you're going to do, I want you to think of me like this. I want you to remember this. I want you to remember the shit and the piss."

I began to speak again, but her look stopped me. There was fury in it, an anger I'd never seen from her before. I turned the car back on and drove us out of the parking lot without saying anything else.

———

When we've finished, Sandra pulls a pack of Marlboros from her jean pocket, lights one. "I thought you quit," I say.

I can't see her face, only the red nub of burn, flaming brighter with each inhalation. "I will," she says.

It is not my business, really. We are not dating. We sleep together secretly. We've not discussed possibilities for the future. I haven't bought her a meal, and she hasn't bought me one. We owe each other nothing, and so I understand that my opinion does not matter, but I can't stop myself from saying, "Those things smell like shit." This is a lie. I've always liked the smell of smoke. I never took up the habit, turned off by the hacking cough it gave me when I tried as a teenager, but through the years I've developed an affinity for the secondhand, for the sharp, crisp burning. I do not know why I've said this to her now, why I put my objection to them on the smell, but I've said it, and I cannot pull it back.

"Then don't smell them," she says. In the dark, I can make out her form shuffling back into her clothes. "I'll see you back there."

I dress and then sit for a time, my back against a pine, and then I stand and move off, away from where the rest of them sit around the fire, listening to the children talk of monsters. The moon is bright, and so I am able to navigate the darkness. After a time, I find myself at the edge of the Vermilion River. Hébert once told me that this marks the end of his property, the water forming a hard border. Someone else's hunting land is on the other side, and I wonder briefly if they are out there tonight too, sitting beside a bonfire. Maybe they are not. Maybe they are at home in their beds. Maybe the woods on the other side are filled only with animals sleeping and prowling.

I slip out of my shoes, roll my pant legs up a bit, and step out into cold river. I think of the creek that ran through my hometown, of the way we'd wade out into it with half-dead logs from its banks each summer. The game was to see who could float on the log longest before sinking it. I had a knack for picking the good ones, the ones that weren't so rotten they'd slip beneath the surface as soon as weight was put on them. Then, the water had been warm, rich, and brown with mud, and it had enveloped us. I wade out farther into the river, letting its water reach up to my thighs. I consider going and rounding up the kids, leading them to the edge of the river, showing them how to play the game. I will not do this. The water is too cold, the darkness too complete. There are likely snakes here. Alligators, even. But I let myself wonder if Mary Ellis could find a good log, one that would keep her afloat.

———

I saw a therapist for a time. We talked mostly about Mary Ellis, about how to help her, and when his questions began to push toward me, I'd admit something small—"I've been thinking of the way she smelled"—rather than admitting something big, and he'd be satisfied that I was forthcoming. I was a good father, worried for his child. The truth is Mary Ellis has handled this better than I have. She's the one who nudges me to bed from the couch, who infects me with her excitement about whatever outing her friends are going on.

There was one conversation with the therapist where I was honest. Surprisingly, my confession came after a question about Mary Ellis. He'd asked me if Mary Ellis was still dreaming of Ellen, something she'd reported to me almost gleefully two weeks after the funeral. She had not been, at least not that she'd told me, but his question made me wonder aloud about the speed with which the world dispatched the real Ellen, the piss-and-shit Ellen. The therapist nodded thoughtfully, asked me to go on.

I told him a story I once read about a man who fell through a grate and into the path of a steam vent, which boiled him alive. He was walking, minding his own business, and as his shoes clanged on the metal grate, he must have felt it start to give, as we all do when we step from concrete to metal, and he must have told himself, *this structure will hold*, as we all do when we step from concrete to metal, and as the grate did give and as he did fall through, he must have thought this was all just a misunderstanding, that the grate itself should have known to support his weight, should have done the thing it was meant to do. Was there bitterness during the boiling? I think there must have been. There must have been the acid knowledge that this was a thing that should not have happened.

I don't think the therapist understood why I was telling him this story, but he smiled thoughtfully, the way he always did, and prodded me to continue. And so, I told him about a day with Ellen, a month before the prognosis, away for a break from our lives, from the fear that had grown in us as we waited on the tests. The two of us went way out to a sandbar. Her skin still held the brown-pink of an early sunburn. I can taste the salt on her shoulders still, can feel the gritty squeeze of her fingers on my arm. That day, I told the therapist, I waded out and reeled in a sand shark, its lithe body whipping against my control. I asked if we should kill it, but Ellen said no. She had me pin its whipping body to the sand while she snipped the hook from its mouth. We jumped back from it before it could swing on us, letting the water pull it back to its home, to the place it was meant to be. We watched it move from the clear, shallow water deeper into the murk, and as her fingernails absently grazed my flesh, I imagined its teeth sinking into her. I reached for her then.

"I think of that day a lot," I told the therapist. "I thought about it as Ellen got sicker. And I wonder now if she thought of it, too, but I never asked."

I told the therapist these things, and he told me with a lot of satisfaction that he really felt like I was dealing with everything in healthy ways, and I nodded and thanked him, but what I really wanted to do was shout at him, to yell that he must stop pretending that the grate had not yet collapsed, that the steam was not yet encasing me, that my life was not yet rising to its sharp, inevitable boil.

———

When I make it back to the fire, Mary Ellis is still talking about her monster. I would have expected the other kids to have lost interest by now, but they're listening intently. Mary Ellis tells us how her monster stalks these woods, how he is part troll and part bear. She gives all the details we could want, talks through the slow dismemberment of deer and rabbits, of children who have wandered too far from home. Her friends make gagging noises and laugh, but Mary Ellis is stone-faced as she relates the details. From the woods, we hear the skittering of feet on leaves. Mary Ellis does not jump, does not even hesitate in her storytelling. She's growing accustomed to this place, to the sounds of harried scrabbling.

"How do we stop your monster?" I ask.

Her face glows in fits and starts, illuminated by the fire I built with Hébert. "You can't stop the monster, Daddy." I wait for an echoing wolf howl, a coyote's seconding call. I want some signifier from the world around us that this moment is nothing but the climax of her story. I want the horror-movie goose bumps of fear to come and then recede, the way they always do, leaving us content in the warm safety of the fire, but from all around us we hear only the pattering voices of our friends and the fearsome silence of a world at peace with what it is.

Blood Heat

This is a story about my hometown, which is to say it is a story about love and about guilt. Belle Reve is a coastal city, one nestled against the Gulf near the Louisiana border. There's a creek that bends itself around the borders of town, its thin dribble of water a belt holding in the strip malls and chain restaurants. The bridges over the creek out into county land don't even really seem like bridges, just continuations of road that happen to cross a trickle of brackish water that feeds into the Gulf at the end of the town's beaches. The meteorologists and climatologists say that in a few decades the creek will overrun the edges of the city, that we'll become something of an island, but in this place people do not acknowledge the reality of their situation.

Belle Reve is growing, has been growing for some years now. Stragglers from the county who stayed in the wilds too long, eager to take jobs at the new beachfront hotels and restaurants mopping floors or else at the tourist traps springing up along the beach highway, have moved in over the last few years. The county people mix and mill with those from the town in all the ways you'd expect. Bar fights increased initially, though they tapered off when each side claimed their own local spots. The old restaurants struggled to stay afloat after the big chains slid in, with their glossy menus and fruity cocktails.

The consolidation of county and city schools was my father's idea. The head coach at the city high school, he sold it to the town aldermen and the county comptroller by showing how much talent his team would have if the county and the city were joined. He promised them championships, and they lobbied the Texas Board of Education, and before long the schools were combined.

Before he was a coach, my father had been a meteorologist. He'd worked for the Air Force during Vietnam, doing work that he never spoke of, and after he came back stateside he went to work for the oil companies, booming in Houston at that time, tracking weather patterns in the Gulf. That's how my family came to this town, seven years before I was born. My father set up a remote office here, to anticipate the effects of hurricanes on the offshore rigs for the Texaco company. Then, the town was undeveloped. There was a little main drag that featured three churches, two banks, a department store, and a smattering of restaurants. The beaches were barren stretches of that rich, brown sand, wild with vegetation. In the early mornings, you could toss a trap into the water with a few chicken necks in it, and by sundown you'd have enough blue crabs for a meal. My mother and I did this frequently those first years. My father would leave for work and the two of us would walk the three blocks to the beach, spend all day browning in the sun before hauling our traps in. My mother barbecued the crabs for dinner, and the three of us would sit around the kitchen table in our first home there, a little bungalow off the main drag, and prize the meat free, our fingers gritted with the seasoning my mother caked onto the outside of the crabs before they went to the grill. In those early days, I didn't understand that there was a world beyond our town's creeks, that there existed places beyond home and beach.

In the last few years, the beaches, once wild with sea oats, have been scraped bare. The aldermen shipped in white tourist sand to cover the gritty brown that caked my boyhood feet. The consolidation happened when I, a freshman, still played JV ball. The talent influx paid off for my father. He made deep playoff runs in those first years, bought a Lexus, convinced the boosters to buy new jerseys and helmets for the Belle Reve High Panthers. Things could have continued like that forever, this town swelling against its border, the outlands overtaking and remaking the place in their own image. The town could have been like any other coastal town, and my father could have made the jump eventually to some large Houston school, or else to the college game as an assistant. All of this could have happened if not for Mard Zaunbrecher.

———

The Mossberg 500 pump-action 12-gauge shotgun is produced in New Haven, Connecticut, by O.F. Mossberg & Sons firearm company. The standard version comes with a stock and regular grip, but it can be upgraded to a pistol grip for a fee. The 500 was originally produced in the 1950s by Carl Benson, Mossberg's lead design engineer during those years. Its stock and pump are made of wood composite that is stained a dark, rich brown. The metal of the barrel and trigger housing is blued. It has a five-shell capacity. While it was originally produced as a hunting weapon, it has since become a popular combat shotgun, and most consumers now report that they purchased their Mossberg 500 pump-action 12-gauge shotgun for home defense.

———

The Zaunbrechers came from the county. The patch of land they lived on sits twenty miles inland. They'd been there for as long as anyone could remember, though using the husks of old vehicles littering the property as a guide, you can tell that they predated the First World War. The Zaunbrecher men had their hands in every county affair, from liquor running to the semi-regular dog fights that took place at an abandoned mill near the edge of the creek bordering town. It was well known that Clay Zaunbrecher was responsible for the death of a Cuban tourist who strayed into the wrong county bar in 1954.

Mard Zaunbrecher was seventeen years old when my father pushed the consolidation, and Mard found himself busing right into the heart of my father's city. He spent that lone year before graduation playing linebacker for my father. My friends and I watched him through hooded eyes, watched him pick fights with other upperclassmen, watched him slide his hand into the jean pockets of girls who also came from the county. We talked to each other of how scary he was, but we each, too, thought of our own hands minnowing their way into denimed crevices, thought of what we'd have become were we Zaunbrechers.

When Mard graduated, he signed up, shipped off to Afghanistan. During those years, I was my father's center on his first two 3A state championship teams. We ran the ball hard those years, and at the end of each game, I dug a divot of grass from the field, slipped it into a baggie, which I kept in my locker.

I left for college the year Mard made it back to the city, to the little string of trailers his grandfather had set up on their farm. None but the old man, Gig Zaunbrecher, lived in the old farmhouse anymore, overrun as it was with a lifetime's detritus. I have seen the interior, have edged through its wink-tight halls. Gig's room sits in the back corner of the house. It is the only room free of clutter and junk. A mattress laid bare on the floor. A lamp. Some old Louis L'Amour westerns.

When he walked into the Belle Reve locker room and asked my father for a job, Mard was changed. The boy I'd watched play for my father just a few years before had been a hothead, thick with muscle, a plug of a guy. Now, muscles still roped his arms, but they were lithe, the kind of muscles you see from car mechanics and machine shop workers, men who use their sinewy limbs for wrench and torque. He was calm now, too. Patient in his explanation of what he wanted from his post-Marine life. My father hired him then as his defensive line coach. In another four years, he became my father's defensive coordinator. He served that role until my father's murder, when he became the interim coach.

———

There is an antique barometer hanging on the kitchen wall of my parents' house. My father purchased it nearly fifty years ago. According to a book I found in his office, a guide to antique weather equipment, this particular barometer was produced for Americans in Dublin in the 1850s and sold through an import company in Boston. It is the shape and size of an ornamented banjo. Wide, round bottom with a clock hand that points to the barometric facts of the moment: Fair, Rainy, Stormy, Very Dry. At the top of the banjo handle there is a thermometer inlaid. My father drained it of mercury long ago, but the numbers are still there, degrees Fahrenheit in increments of ten. Next to the hash mark that would represent 98.6, some Irish craftsman had etched the words "Blood Heat" on a small metal plate.

———

I played three years of college ball at Texas Tech, out across the state in Lubbock. In my junior year, I tore every tendon and ligament in my left knee. For a time, I lost feeling in the limb, and the doctors told me that I might lose it, but the feeling returned, and after months of rehab, I was able to walk on it again. Still, my playing days were done, and so I threw myself into school. These days, I live in Mississippi, where I teach English and coach a team of my own. We are not so good as my father's teams, but my players work hard, and I enjoy standing on the sidelines on a warm fall evening, playing at strategy, testing myself against the mind of the coach across the way.

Mard was a good defensive coordinator for my father, though they had some fundamental disagreements from the start. My father ran the 4-2-5, a defense that uses a roving fifth defensive back in a hybrid role instead of having a third linebacker. Mard did not believe in the 4-2-5. Probably correctly, he believed that the talent in the Belle Reve area would adapt better to the 3-4. Home for visits, I saw the two of them argue this point companionably many times over beer at the beachfront bar my father frequented.

———

Hurricanes, my father once told me, are more dangerous slow than fast. Speed and power can do immediate damage, he said. They can knock down power lines and wash out beachfront pilings. They can uproot trees and make a show of their strength, but they are not the ones to fear. It is the slow hurricane, no matter its power, that threatens everything. If it is slow, my father said, it will cycle and stall, sucking more and more water to dump, causing flooding that damages the structures built to withstand the wind and force of the faster storms. When Harvey hit Houston three years ago, when the storm stalled over east Texas, when the highways and interstates ran deep as rivers, my father called me to tell me that he'd been right. It is the slow storm, he said, that kills you.

———

The year that my father died, Belle Reve dropped its first three games. My father's air raid offense put up plenty of points, but the defense could not stop anyone. Teams gashed them on the ground. I followed the team's performance vaguely. I had my own team to worry about, my own life with its own petty worries and troubles, and so on a Friday night of Belle Reve's first bye week of the season, I was not expecting the message from my mother, telling me that my father had not come home, that he was not answering his phone. I did not call her back that night. I'd just finished a two-overtime loss of my own, and I did not have it in me to think about home or my parents right then. Instead, I sat in my quiet house, replaying the game in my mind, doing the old coach's work of second-guessing each decision. My father once told me that at times like that, he just had to order his mind to turn off. I have never had that ability.

———

When I was ten, I took one of my father's small barometers to school for a science presentation. The barometer was small, made of brass and glass, and it was carried in a round leather case about the size of a hatbox. Near the lid's latch was a small hole, looped with a ring made of the same brass as the barometer. My father explained to me that this hole was to allow a free flow of air into the case when the barometer was put away. He explained how delicate an instrument like this could be. Sitting in the back of the classroom, waiting on my turn, I fidgeted with the case, slid a finger through the brass ring and into the case. When I tried to remove my finger, I found that it was stuck tight. My knuckle would not come back through the hole it had slipped through, and so I carried the case attached to my hand the rest of the day, deflected teacher questions, ignored the jokes of friends, finally showed my father. He used soft, warm butter to ease the swollen joint free. The leather surrounding the brass ring on the case—which sits on the shelf above my father's desk—is still dark with the stain of that grease.

———

My mother and I drove to the Lufkin game together. The Belle Reve stadium sits a block east of the high school, three blocks off the beach road. From the stands, you can smell the salt. We took our seats, accepted condolences with lip-tight nods. At some point in the pregame ritual, we were recognized over the PA system, asked to stand. We received the claps, returned to our seats, awaited the game. My father was buried the day before. The casket was closed, but when I arrived in town, the funeral home let me look at him. The buckshot had taken a piece of his chest, most of his neck, a portion of his chin. On the field, Mard wore the same headset my father had worn. That night, Mard's newly installed 3-4 defense did not stop Lufkin's option running attack.

The 3-4 defense was popularized in the NFL in the late 1970s. It fell out of favor, though, replaced by the 4-3 that was used by the great Mike Ditka Bears teams of the mid-80s. It made a return in the early 2000s, though, when its success at the college level began to bleed upward. That bleed works back and forth, with innovation moving up from high school to college to NFL, then NFL popularity bleeding back downward, infesting the college and high school games. My father tried to resist such trends. He believed in molding his plans based on more local factors: What was his talent capable of? Which schemes would work best with the players at his disposal? What were his opponents going to attempt? Could he forecast their plans and react accordingly?

I sat across my father's desk from Mard. At his elbow sat a box with my father's personal effects from the office.

"He sure was a good man," Mard said.

I looked at my feet. "He was."

"This has been rough as hell on the team. All I can do to keep them playing."

"They'll be alright. Dad always said a little adversity is good for a team."

"He was right," Mard said.

"How's the switch to the 3-4 going?"

"Very well, very well. Kids are taking to it. I tell you what, we got this kid, a nose tackle, he can knock the piss out of a center. Going to really make our defense proactive."

"Proactive," I said.

"Your dad, he liked to plan for what the offense was gonna do. 4-2-5's good for that, for thinking about their plan and then adjusting to it. I guess I'm more thinking of our defense as action-based, instead of reaction-based, if you get my meaning."

I nodded.

Did I know then? There's no telling. But when I stood and took the box from him, I found myself looking at his hands, as if searching for some spatter, some evidence of the thing.

————

The night Mard Zaunbrecher killed my father, the wind was blowing in from the northwest at 35 miles per hour. In Oakland, José Altuve hit two home runs to help the Astros top the Athletics in game four of the American League Championship Series. Somewhere over the Atlantic, the president slept aboard Air Force One on his way to the G8 summit. Around about when Mard's Mossberg kicked and my father died, I was giving my pregame speech. I don't remember what I told my team. I do not write these things down. I know that we played Moss Point in a light fog and that a weather pattern that would eventually spin a tornado into Montgomery, Alabama, was just forming in the long flatness of west Texas, and the air in Belle Reve was a chilly 55 degrees, but my father was in his shirt sleeves when he died. He'd have had goose bumps, I'm sure. Sometime near when he was murdered, a high school girlfriend of mine was posting a racist meme on Facebook that would set off a long string of argumentative comments from all our old acquaintances, and a new episode of *20/20* was airing with an exposé on a network of car dealerships that were bilking customers of their service fees, and all around the world hearts continued to beat, but in Laughlin County, Texas, my father's heart was shredded by buckshot at Mard Zaunbrecher's hands.

Mard's Mossberg is in the evidence room of the Laughlin County Sheriff's Department. I have seen it, have hefted its weight, have looked long at the blued barrel, at the metal channels along which the pump slides. They hold too much grease from the gun's last oiling. I have felt the trigger weight, which is lighter than you'd think. It would not have taken any pressure at all for Mard to pull the trigger.

The night my father died, Mard picked him up from the fieldhouse, where he was watching game film to prep for Lufkin. I do not know what Mard told him to get him in the truck. I do not know what they spoke of on the long drive to Mard's family land, out in the county. I do not know what Mard said to get him out of the truck. I do not know what my father's final words were, and I do not know if he knew what was coming or if he was surprised. He'd have seen the gun, I'm sure, for the wounds were not in his back.

Weeks later, detectives from the sheriff's department would find bits of my father's bloody shirt turned down into a deeper layer of manure. They have told me that Mard shot him in this spot, that his body bucked backward into the pile, that it looks like Mard turned the manure, folded the traces of my father down into the pile after he hauled my father's body to the bed of his truck.

Mard dumped my father's body at the creek's edge. It was found the next morning by two boys, both eleven years old. They were walking alongside the creek, wearing their fathers' army fatigues, pretending at a war march, when they came across what was left of my father. They ran back home. They found the body at about 10:30 a.m., which would have been the same time I was telling my mother—after finally returning her call—that I was sure my father was fine, that he probably drank one too many beers on the bye week and hadn't been able to drive home. I did not believe this, even then, but I was hoping.

———

My father quit his work as a meteorologist when I was ten years old. He and my mother had saved, had bought our house outright, had prepared for him to seek out his passion. The job posting at Belle Reve High asked for a science teacher who could also coach some sports. On his first day of work that fall, my mother and I presented him with a silver whistle, wrapped in tight red ribbon. Though he left the work behind, my father still kept his home equipment. Functioning barometers, hygrometers, anemometers. For years he charted patterns, kept meticulous notes. It was what he did to unwind from the stresses of coaching. The last time we spoke, he warned me that a front would be blowing through my area of north Mississippi, that I should plan for inside practices that week, though the local forecasts were for sun each afternoon. He was right. My players spent that Tuesday afternoon in rough contact within our gymnasium while outside the rain fell and the thunder echoed their collisions.

———

Movies and books would have you believe that there would be some revelation, some detective's breakthrough that could lead to the criminal's capture. This is not true. The investigation was going nowhere when Mard's cousin Feather, beset with guilt, drove to the sheriff's department and told them who had done the crime.

Feather was a defensive back on the same teams I'd played on. Like his cousin, Feather came from the county. He was raised on the Zaunbrecher land. He played four years at Sam Houston State and became an FCS All-American before he came back and got a job on the rigs. As far as I could tell, the only things he liked in this world were beer, weed, and the kind of chaos ball that would result in defensive backs getting lots of interceptions.

I have been told hat when the investigators asked Feather why he came forward, he looked down at his hands before giving a grunting shrug.

———

Look to the Gulf. You can see there the oil rigs in the distance, hazy through the early morning cloud cover. Smell deeply of the air. Remove socks and shoes, roll up pant legs, feel the powdery, white sand beneath your feet. Walk here at the water's edge. The forecasts tell you that there is a tropical storm already brewing in the Atlantic, the first of the season. Think of your father's work, think of the tracking of threats, the preparation for damage that cannot be dodged. Walk further, waving to early morning joggers and dog walkers. You will leave soon. *I'll give thee a wind*. You will teach, and you will coach, but for the moment walk in this soft, clean sand, taste the salt breeze. After a time, reach the creek's slow trickle into the Gulf. Stand there in the margins, braced against the flow that comes from the Brazos and the Red River before that. Imagine the storm that is brewing, imagine this water bubbling with rainfall, rising as the slow storm bears down. Imagine this place falling to the inevitable. In your anger and your shame, stand firm in that ceaseless water.

Snowless Winter Abecedarian

Again, the porch is humid-slick. Before you came here to Louisiana you assumed humidity was for summers, the thick weight of watered air clogging your lungs on early morning runs. Can you be blamed for thinking a change in seasons would also bring a change in humidity? December is here now, and the cold burrows deep. Each night, you sit on the porch with Tara, and though it feels cold enough to snow, all you get is the same moist air. Friends warned you, told you that the cold cuts deeper where there is moisture, but you came anyway.

"Growing up without snowball fights is unnatural," you tell Tara.

"How many crawfish boils did you get as a kid?" she asks. Instead of answering, you reach a hand to her stomach, taut and round now. "Just promise me we won't ever move to the great frozen North," she says.

Kids were not part of the plan when you came from Indiana, but the two of you have found yourselves with one on the way, a girl. Long ago, your father muttered a curse, telling you that you're doomed to have a child as troubling as you were. More than being afraid, though, you find yourself anxious. "Nothing can prepare you for this," your father said when you told him that he would be a grandfather sometime in late spring. Of course, you knew that nothing could prepare you.

"Perish the thought," you finally say to Tara. "Question, though. Are you sure we're ready for this? Sometimes I feel like we just figured out who we are, and now we're going to throw a kid in the mix."

Tara looks at you for a long beat. You regret bringing this up immediately, sure that you've upset her. "Very sure," she says, finally, with a smile, and you feel let off the hook.

"What about a name?" she questions, a move in the conversation she takes each night on the porch.

"Xanadu," you say immediately, an old joke to the two of you now, a name that you threw out in desperation weeks ago, when you felt that all other possibilities had been exhausted. You have thought long about a name, the both of you have, and there's been a gradual winnowing of possibilities, all the Jennifers and Lindas and Susies nixed from the running mental list, but as you run your feet across the water-slicked concrete of the porch, inspiration strikes, and you feel for the first time certain that the two of you can make this work, that you can become parents who do not fail their child, or at least who do not fail their child in such a way that the damage is irreparable, because in this moment, in the moment before naming, you find yourself longing to hold a small hand, to brush drifting pollen from a towhead.

"Zoe?" you say, and as you say it, you know that the name is right, that your Zoe will run through these humid winters and summers, that she will catch lightning bugs in her sweat-sheened fists, that she will pinch the tails and suck the heads, that she will find in her voice a drawl that her mother comes by naturally and that you, only recently, have found creeping into your own voice, a change that in this moment makes you certain that a place can change you and that those changes can be, with a little luck, for the better.

Brothers

Noseeum was deep into his third year of working the rig when the email from Smith, his eldest and only surviving brother, arrived. He was sitting in the lounge area, drinking a cup of black coffee that had already gone cold in the blasting AC. The lone computer that was available for personal use was old and slow, its keys grimy. He logged in, and in the middle of spam messages and advertisements was his brother's email. The subject line read simply, "Come home."

It had been a long day for Noseeum. His hand had slipped while tightening a bolt, and the wrench had spun from his grasp, rapping his knee solidly. Later, he'd scraped a swath of skin from one knuckle. To top it off, the boys were making catfish in the kitchenette, and he found the sick smell of old grease cloying. His first thought was that his brother wanted him to come home for a visit, to come see all the nieces and nephews. His brother and his wife had produced a thick brood, all towheaded like Noseeum's father had been. Christmas had been the last time he'd made it back, and that was months ago. He knew he was due for another visit, but he was only really interested in spending his next three weeks off sitting in his little studio apartment, drinking beer and trying to sleep with his neighbor, who broke up with her boyfriend the weekend before Noseeum left for this three-week shift. He clicked the email.

This is Ruth. Smith died this morning. Please come home.

Noseeum typed out a fast reply. He did not ask his brother's wife how his brother had died. There would be time enough for the details once he got off the rig, got back to a place with cell phone service. Instead, he told her he was coming, that he would be there as soon as he could, that they should not hold the funeral without him.

He spoke with his supervisor, who spoke with the bosses, who called in another worker to take Noseeum's place. It was not the kind of thing they normally did, but Noseeum was a good employee, the type who was never late, who never overslept his shift, who cleaned up after himself and didn't complain, and so they let him leave the next morning.

He hurriedly packed a bag, bought a plane ticket, Lake Charles-to-Houston-to-Chicago. He left his car in the lot of the Lake Charles airport. It was, thankfully, a small enough place to not charge for short or long term. It was only when he'd gotten through security, found himself seated on the plane, which was taxiing to the runway, that he realized he hadn't called his sister-in-law or mother to find out the details.

His layover in Houston afforded him only enough time to rush from one gate to the next, and so it wasn't until he landed in Chicago that he called to find out what had happened to his older brother. A car wreck. Dead on impact.

———

Noseeum's family lived on a farm deep in the woods of northern Indiana. His parents had wanted a girl, had kept trying for a girl, producing the first three brothers spread across a six-year gap before they received the news that the newest baby would also be a boy. He, Noseeum, the last straw, was born on the first day of March in the midst of an uncommon snowstorm. Smith, his eldest brother, had to care for the younger siblings while his parents drove the thirty minutes to the hospital. He was born early, underweight, and above average for height, a bean pole whom the brothers immediately began to call "Noseeum" for the way he seemed always to buzz about them, even before he could walk. The name stuck throughout his childhood, persisting even into his preteen years when he finally thickened, his gaunt face turning chubby, his bosoms beginning to fill. He had a rosy-cheeked moon face that his mother adored and his friends mocked. By the time he left for the army at eighteen, he had come to tolerate the teasing nickname, and by the time he returned, both of his middle brothers were dead, and he found himself liking the nickname.

In the army, Noseeum's body finally found its balance, hardening into a mass of sinew and tendon. He did not tell any of his comrades about his nickname, and so they called him by his given name, which was pleasant enough for him, though boring. He'd come to expect the sound of his name to carry some fraught connotation, but during basic and then during the long months of his first tour of duty, stationed at a remote outpost in northern Afghanistan, he found himself growing contemptuous of his real name. When he took a bullet to the calf and was discharged, he found himself working three-week-on/three-week-off shifts on an oil rig in the Gulf of Mexico, and the first thing he told his coworkers was to call him Noseeum. They laughed at this, but they obliged, and he again felt like he was at home.

Smith had come first, had been the start of the eight-year run of boys every other year. He was followed by Dennis, Laremy, and Noseeum himself.

Their father grew corn and soy in alternating years. He'd inherited the land from an uncle, took it over at twenty, married the boys' mother, and began to raise the family.

They lived in an Italianate farmhouse built in the 1890s. It was tall and columned, with shining hardwood floors that the boys' mother hollered about whenever a scratch or nick appeared, which was often, given the tendency of young boys to do things like try to juggle pocketknives.

The boys helped on the farm and rode the bus into La Porte for school. They did not stick to themselves or find an uncommon bond amongst them. They each had friends in their every-other-year grades, and they grew as children grow, sometimes resentful of their siblings, sometimes loyal.

The older brothers picked on Noseeum, complained about his hovering, but they also taught him to fashion fishing lures from corn husks and trained him on how to talk to girls when he confessed at nine to having a crush on Cindy Carson.

It was known in the family from the start that Smith would take over the farm, and when their father died during the summer of Noseeum's thirteenth year, that is what happened. Smith had not left home when he graduated. He'd already married Ruth, whom he'd dated off-and-on throughout middle and high school. They'd lived the first year of their marriage in the converted hayloft of the old barn, and when the boys' father died, their mother moved to the loft and Smith and Ruth took over the master bedroom of the farmhouse. That summer was an uncommon one for stink bugs. There were always swarms of the things in May and June, but that year they lingered until nearly August, creeping into the house through cracks and nooks, wandering aimlessly across the window units the boys' mother insisted they only use in the deepest part of the afternoon.

Noseeum spent the summer of his father's death like he spent all his summers, working the land, fixing machinery, hauling and lifting and doing the things that first his father and then Smith told him to do. In the late afternoons he wandered the thick woods that bracketed their land. Sometimes he picked mushrooms, and sometimes he swatted flies, and sometimes he found crooks of fallen trees to nap on. At dinner time, he sat in his usual spot and ate the usual food, though now it was sometimes cooked by Ruth instead of his mother. Reality recalibrated itself, and Noseeum adjusted.

———

Noseeum did not recognize his mother's hayloft apartment. In the time he'd been gone, she'd redecorated, shuffling the furniture around the big room, setting up dividers to hide her bed and bath, and hanging large canvas prints with portraits of his dead brothers and father along one pine wall. Noseeum stood in front of the portraits of Dennis and Laremy. She'd chosen pictures from close to their teen years. Dennis's was a school picture, his hair swept flopping across his brow. On the blown-up picture, Noseeum could clearly see a smatter of pimples across the bridge of his nose. He wondered, briefly, when Smith had last had a picture taken. He'd never really been the type. Would his mother dig out an old school photo for him too? A candid shot?

From behind him came the clattering of dishes. "Mom," he said, "really, I'm not hungry."

"I made this pasta salad two days ago, and if you don't eat it, it'll never get finished."

He sat. He'd arrived just minutes before to find the farm deserted. He poked through the house, looking for Ruth or one of his nieces or nephews, for someone, but it was silent and empty, the rooms still. He'd forgotten what that could be like. In Louisiana, the heat required constant AC, constant motion, even if unseen. In the farmhouse, he remembered suddenly what it was like to be in a room where nothing moved, save yourself. He'd left his bag in the living room and walked out past the new barn, down the gravel path to the old barn. He'd found his mother there, in her apartment, Swiffering the floors.

Now, she spooned a helping of pasta salad into his bowl, set a fork beside it, and looked at him expectantly. He wasn't hungry, found himself with no appetite at all, but he took a bite, smiled at her.

"Where are Ruth and the kids?" he asked.

"Ruth's in town. Taking care of all the arrangements."

"Alone?"

"Father Tim's there with her."

"You didn't want to go?"

His mother waved her hand dismissively. "The kids are all staying with friends."

Noseeum took another bite. His mother, sitting at the table next to him, flexed her hands. She had long, thin fingers. Piano-player fingers. He'd inherited his father's frame, fingers included. "How are you holding up, Mom?"

She looked out the window and didn't speak for a time. He reached over, took her hand in his. "I'm okay," she said. "Eat your pasta salad. It'll get cold."

"It's pasta salad. It's supposed to get cold."

"But that's the thing you say, right?" She stood from the table. "That's the thing the mother says to the son who she's feeding after a long trip. 'Eat your food before it gets cold.'"

Noseeum ate his pasta salad, and they waited there together for Ruth and the kids.

———

Dennis was the first to die. A hothead from the time he was a young child, he was well known in the La Porte bars as a fighter, someone likely to drink a few beers and look for trouble. It was in one of these bars that, at twenty-two years of age, he picked a fight with an amateur MMA fighter who took him to the ground quickly, applied a choke hold, and did not let up quickly enough. Dennis never regained consciousness, despite the machines and tubes and cluck-clucking of doctor tongues, and eventually everyone accepted that he would never come back. This was during the spring of Noseeum's senior year in high school. He'd already signed on with the army, pending his graduation. Those long weeks before Dennis eventually succumbed and left them were a blur to Noseeum now. He'd loved Dennis, had loved him in the way the youngest brother often loves a middle sibling, connected by the oddity of their positions in the family. He sat afternoons when school let out for long hours in the hospital beside Dennis's bed. The doctors and nurses encouraged him to talk to Dennis, to tell him stories and sing his favorite songs. "He can hear you in there," they'd say, again and again. "It doesn't seem like it, but he can." Noseeum did not tell him stories, though, and he did not sing his favorite songs. He sat, a part of him believing that if Dennis could hear the stories and songs, he could also sense his presence in other ways. A kind of radar, Noseeum thought. *He knows I'm here. He can feel me.* Dennis died in the early morning hours of a Saturday, weeks before Noseeum graduated and shipped off to basic training. He was there for the funeral, at least, there to stand beside his brothers and mother.

———

Late in the evening, after Ruth and the children returned, after tears and hugs and bedtime stories read by Uncle Noseeum, after several drinks at the edge of the field behind the farmhouse, Ruth told Noseeum what happened to Smith. "We had a fight," she said. "You know how he could be. Sensitive. He'd never show it, but when he was hurt, he felt it all the way, you know?"

Noseeum did know. He'd seen it all his life. Smith, the one in charge, the one who took care of everything, was also the one who would recoil at the harsh words. When Noseeum was five or six, their father had hollered "Don't be an idiot" at Smith as they worked on the tractor, and Smith had gone silent, his eyes glazed, and Noseeum, sitting off to the side, playing war with a handful of nails in the dirt, watched his brother stand awkwardly and walk away from their father. It took days for Smith to return to normal, for the looseness to come back to his joints, for his voice to regain its command and clarity.

"It's not your fault," Noseeum said to Ruth.

"He wouldn't have been driving if we hadn't had a fight. He always drove after, and then he'd come back, and we'd make up, once he'd felt the hurt a while."

"But that doesn't mean it was your fault."

"I didn't make that deer run out in front of him, you mean. No. I guess in that way, it's not my fault."

They each took a sip from their drinks, and Noseeum looked out at the field. The soy was coming in well, thick and low to the ground. Nicely green, he'd noticed that afternoon. Back in Lake Charles, in the deep summer months, there was the stench of wet, rotting vegetation everywhere. The plants were a weighty green that felt almost viscous.

"What are you going to do with the farm?" Noseeum said.

"Not now for questions, Noseeum. Not yet, please."

"OK," he said. He wanted to tell her he would help, that he could stay and work the land, but he'd never had Smith's knack or desire for the work. The air was cool, no humidity at all, and he took in a big lungful of it, wanting to remember this moment, this feeling, when he returned to Lake Charles.

Laremy's diagnosis came swiftly during Noseeum's second month in Afghanistan, and he was gone by the time the fifth month came. Noseeum learned of the diagnosis in an email and of the death in a hazy video call, which he couldn't remember even five minutes after the call ended. He drank hooch that night, drank himself dumb, but he did not tell anyone what had happened or why he was drinking or crying or cursing. He woke for reveille to find crude drawings Sharpied on his face and arms, and even then he did not tell anyone that his brother had died. He emailed Smith to tell him that he could not come home for the funeral, which was likely true, though Noseeum did not ask. Two weeks later, Laremy freshly in the ground, Noseeum took the bullet to the calf and found himself sent first to a hospital in Germany and then back home. His brother was not a month dead when he walked with crutches into the graveyard and stood before his tombstone. Laremy, the closest in age to Noseeum, had been both his first friend and his first enemy. They'd fought violently as young boys, Laremy glad to finally have someone smaller to command and Noseeum eager to prove that though he was the smallest, he was not so small as to be inconsequential. They'd been close, too, though, in the way of brothers who have tested one another, and standing above his grave, Noseeum felt something he could not describe come over him. He threw up in the grass beside the grave and went back to the farm, where he recovered from his injury. He left for Lake Charles, a place he had never been, as soon as he was able.

———

The day after Smith's funeral, Noseeum sat in the farmhouse kitchen with his mother and Ruth, drinking coffee. "I'll need to get back to the rig soon," he said.

Ruth nodded. "We know."

"I don't mean to run off on you guys. Just have to get back." His mother stood without speaking, carried her coffee mug to the sink, and rinsed it.

"I'll come back at Thanksgiving."

"We'll be here," Ruth said.

Noseeum's mother walked outside, and after a moment, Noseeum followed her. They sat together on the back porch, looking out across the soy, and she finally said, "For years I marked time with you boys. First having you and then later all the little milestones. Birthdays and T-ball and proms."

Noseeum took her hand. Its skin seemed papery now, but there was still strength in it, the hard grip of her life's labor. "You'll still have that with the kids. Ruth's going to need you."

His mother withdrew her hand. She looked at him, and for the first time in his life, he felt real anger coming from her. "I don't think you understand what you just said to me. I don't think you do at all."

"I'm sorry, Mom."

"I wasn't nattering on about all those milestones because I want to relive them. I was trying to find a way to explain that now the milestones are death. Your father and then all your brothers, and you'll be next. Or Ruth. Or, heaven forbid, the children. Do you know what that's like? To measure your life by the loss of the people you love most?"

Noseeum didn't respond. He wanted to tell her that he did, that the loss of his father, his brothers, affected him in this way, too, but he understood suddenly that this was not true. He felt the loss of each of them, but this emotion she was trying to explain to him was something he didn't feel, couldn't feel in the way she did.

"I'm sorry," he said again. "I won't leave yet. I'll . . ." He couldn't finish the thought. He felt himself suddenly craving the Louisiana heat, the oppressive weight of it. Just walking from door to car, you'd feel yourself slick with sweat, your chest anchored by the humidity. Why did he want that? Why did he want a thing that felt so counter to who he was, where he was from?

He stood, put a hand briefly on her shoulder, and walked away. In the distance, across the big field, the tops of the trees moved in the breeze, and Noseeum thought again of Louisiana, where the trees did not move all summer, it seemed, sunk under the weight of still air. In the driveway, he heard his nieces and nephews hollering at one another, and so he walked to where they sat in the dirt, playing. There were five of them, aged out at two-year intervals just as he and his siblings had been. They sat in a cluster, arguing loudly over whose toy was whose and who got a turn first with this toy or that, and he thought of walking to them, telling them that they should not fight, should never fight because life was fleeting and hard and the time they had together, this time, this moment in the driveway in the dirt, would be gone so quickly it would astonish them. He did not walk over, and he did not say this. Instead, he walked slowly to the edge of the driveway, to a very old tree, the first tree he climbed as a boy, and he leaned back against its trunk, and he watched the little group argue and play, watched the way those two elements of their lives blended so seamlessly together. They were laughing one minute and hollering the next. He ran his fingers along the blackened bark of the tree. It had been struck by lightning when Noseeum was a child, and neighbors had urged his father to take it down, telling him that it would never survive, but it was far enough from the house and barn that if it fell, it would not harm anything, and so his father had simply sawed off the limbs that had taken a direct hit from the lightning and left the rest of the tree, which did not die. It grew, winding still, up above Noseeum, its leaves a mild green, and though there were gaps here and there, spaces where the burned limbs once covered the sky, the tree itself stood.

Robards + Redbarn

My daddy was a middle linebacker. In my earliest memories, he is a force, flinging himself sideline to sideline. He never got to have a name on his jersey (Coach Turner didn't allow it), and after watching him play every week for years, I associated his number, 49, with his name—our name—Robards. I'd sit in the stands, watching him feint up, faking a blitz, and I'd know that number 49 was my daddy, that it was my daddy bringing down Brown and Swann and all the other greats.

After the games, we would eat together at Jimmy's, a steakhouse near the Arrowhead where we were given a back-corner booth, a place where we wouldn't be disturbed by fans. Sometimes other players joined us, and sometimes we ate on our own. We'd eat our rib eyes and talk football. My mother hated that I went to the games and to places where the other players were, but I hardly ever saw her, and she knew better than to suggest I stop going.

"Wilma," my father would say, his spoon hovering, full of mashed potatoes, "did you see when I got that sack?"

"On a blitz."

"Right. And what kind of coverage were we running?"

"Zone," I'd say, sawing the weighty steak knife into my meat, thinking that if I kept eating like this maybe I'd get strong enough to play ball, even if I was a girl. "Two men high."

Now, I'm standing on the practice field at Our Lady of the Annunciation, watching my friend Kevin hit a tackling dummy, and I know better. We are just friends, Kevin and I. Up until a year or two ago, we hadn't ever even talked. Then, he figured out that of the kids in our class, I knew the most about football. He figured out who my father was and that I could teach him things he needs to know if he's ever going to really play. This school is expensive, but my father still has enough money left to pay the tuition.

In a year, when I'm sixteen, the team has said they'll give me a part-time job in the front office. Fetching coffee. Delivering mail. It's a job that my father lined up for me when he was still playing. Most of my classmates won't get jobs at all. They'll drive their shiny new cars, drink together at bars that aren't supposed to serve them, but I'll spend my free time in the GM's office, helping Ms. Linda, the old secretary who's been there for as long as I've been alive.

"Again," I say to Kevin, and he springs forward, wraps up the tackling dummy, brings it down. Once he's off it, the dummy pops back upright, bobbing a little bit.

I have him come at the dummy from different angles, different distances, at different speeds until he's drenched in sweat. When I finally give him a water break, he sits in the grass in front of me, and says, "You hear about Redbarn?"

Trenton Redbarn took my father's place on the team when my father quit playing two years ago. He's not as good as my father was, but he's a sideline-to-sideline defender, and the team only spent a seventh-round pick on him. Kevin knows that he's my favorite player. He knows that at games, I shout his name almost as much as I shout "Chiefs." He doesn't know that at night, I close my eyes, pretend that Redbarn is there with me. He doesn't know that in the few times I've met Redbarn, I've imagined myself older, him younger, the two of us together on the little mattress in my room, he in his full pads, his helmet still attached.

"What's happening with Redbarn?" I ask.

"Getting traded is what I heard. On the radio this morning."

"They say if it was for sure? Is it done?"

He shakes his head. "I don't know, Wilma. Would suck. He's really at the edge of getting good."

I close my eyes. I know that Kevin needs me to get him up, get him going on the next drill to help him develop, but I don't know how to react to this news. It shouldn't bother me. Players get traded. But there is something more to this, something I can't make sense of, and so I keep my eyes closed, even after Kevin says my name.

———

My father is awake when I get back to our house. It's only five in the afternoon, but he's been sleeping more and more lately. Now, though, he's sitting at the desk in his study, huddled over his little lap chalkboard. I sit down beside him.

"Daddy," I say, "what's happened with Redbarn?"

"He's a Mike linebacker," he says, his hand still moving the chalk across the board.

From the trash can next to his desk, I pull the paper out, flip to the column about yesterday's game. Redbarn turned in an unremarkable performance. A handful of tackles, not much more. As I scan the pages, I don't see anything about a trade. "I heard he's gone."

"I played the Mike, too."

I reach over to him, touch his shoulder. Sometimes contact helps bring him back, and I hope that now, for this conversation, he'll come back at least a little bit. "Is Redbarn getting traded? Have you heard anything?"

My father turns away from the play he's scribbling. His eyes are leaking fluid, and for a moment I think he's crying for Redbarn, but I know that this is just excess moisture, that his eyes do this now. I hand him a cloth.

"Is that a new play, Daddy?"

"It's a man/zone mix," he says, smiling. This is his life now, scribbling out plays that he takes over to the football complex once a week. He doesn't go to practice or games. He sits at his desk, hunched over the chalkboard, scribbling until he lands on something he likes. He transfers those plays to bits of paper, which he takes to Coach Turner, trying to piece together a game plan that probably won't be used. The team put him on salary, though it's far less than he made as a player, far less than any of the coaches or support staff make. "I'm dropping a defensive end into coverage in case of a slant."

"Sounds like a good one," I say, standing. At Our Lady, we read all the works that they say are important in our classes, but on my own time, I work my way through my father's dense shelf of football books. As a girl, I would scan the titles relentlessly, settling on ones at random, letting myself sink into the schemes and formations, the moves and countermoves. My father let me do this, let me sit in his study for hours, bent over the books, trying to parse meaning from the symbols on the page. Some days, before he stopped playing, he'd sit with me, read whichever one I'd selected that day. Nights in my room, I'd trace formations in my coloring books as he showed me how to adjust them. We'd read through the explanations of the option or the pistol, and he'd show me why one formation can be better than another. These days, I'm more methodical. I've been studying his guides to technique, to help with my coaching of Kevin.

When I was younger, I'd visit my mother sometimes at her house in Mississippi, where she lives with my younger brother and her new husband, but those were days and nights to be tolerated. There, in her sterile house, I never felt at home the way I do here, with my father. Even after the last bell ringer, after the hospitalization, after the days of worrying about paralysis, after he was forced to stop playing, forced into his current role, I refused to move down there with them. She doesn't know the extent of the damage—I've shielded him from that—but it's only a matter of time before he spirals further downward, before the balance we've attained ends.

I walk down the carpeted hallway to my room. It's a corner room, windows looking out into our back and side yards. My bed, covered in a Chiefs bed set, is situated against the back wall, next to the window. I was three when we moved to this house in Deer Valley. My father had been playing for the Chiefs a few years already, and my parents had split, my mother gone back to her hometown. At that age, I think I spent equal time with the two of them. That was more than a decade ago, and my memories of coming to this place are hazy. In the intervening years, Deer Valley, with its modest homes, has become popular with Chiefs players. More than a dozen players live here. I see them, now and again, out on the streets or at the expansive park that sits tucked into one corner of the community, bracketed by thick woods.

I lie down on my bed, face the wall. Beside the window I've carved *Robards + Redbarn*, dug it deep into the drywall. At night, staring at those words, I think of myself and Redbarn. In my mind my muscles pulse and throb, and I imagine the two of us tackling some running back together, the force of our motion colliding. When I think these things, I imagine us falling to the turf, the running back disappearing, Redbarn huddled against me on the perfectly manicured grass.

I close my eyes and try to picture us there, together, but I can't form a coherent image. Redbarn shifts and disappears in my mind, and when I look at myself I don't see the woman I thought I'd be, I see the girl I am, too small, drowning in the pads and jersey.

I think of Redbarn packing up his things, moving to some new city, some new team. I have seen this before, of course, seen players sign new deals or get traded or retire, but there always seemed to be an orderliness to it. Thinking about it now, I cannot figure what value the team will get from trading Redbarn, can't understand why they'd make this move now.

Kevin came with me to the game on Sunday, sat with me in my father's seats. From the first snap, I called out the plays, explaining formations and alignments to Kevin, trying to prepare him for next spring's tryouts, when he'll have another chance to make the team. He tried last year, but that was before I was coaching him. On Sunday, Coach Turner blitzed Redbarn all game, sent him from his spot there in the middle to try to break through. I recognized my father's schemes, the complicated blitz packages that he helped to put together for himself years ago.

My father's schemes didn't work on Sunday, though. The Chiefs lost 14–0 to the Browns. After the game, I kept my eyes on Redbarn. He walked around the field, shaking hands, slapping backs. He was fine, not even a trace of a limp from the low ankle sprain he'd had earlier in the season.

I try again to imagine a reason why they would trade him. I get up off the bed, walk back down the hallway to my father's study. He is still at work on the play, fussing over the zones his linebackers will cover. "I'm going out for a bit," I say.

He doesn't look up, doesn't say anything as I leave the room. I do not have my license, but I've been driving my father's Cadillac for the last six months. At first, it was out of necessity. Pantry bare, my father unable to do the shopping that day, and no desire on my part to loop my mother in, I got myself to the grocery. Now, I drive whenever I feel like it. In the car, without even thinking, I start the drive out to the Chiefs' practice facility, where the team must be wrapping up their afternoon.

———

The wide hallways of the Chiefs' offices are papered with pictures of KC greats. At the edge of the doorway to the VP's office, there's a framed picture of my father. He's standing up from sacking Terry Bradshaw in a Chiefs playoff win from nearly a decade ago. His arms hang by his side, weighty with muscle. Through his facemask, you can see a wide grin spread across his face. If you could zoom in, enhance the picture, you would see, I'm sure, tiny cracks etched across the surface of his helmet.

I never have a problem getting in here. The guards at the gate know me, wave me through. They could probably get in trouble for this, but I never cause problems while I'm here, never bother any of the players or executives, so they let me do it—out of kindness or pity, I'm not sure which.

I'm standing in the hallway, thinking about my father as he was then, as he is now, when I feel a tap on my shoulder. As I turn, I'm taken in by a hug, thick and weighty.

"Let me go, Freeman." He backs up a step, but I still have to look up to see his face. He's still in his practice gear, and when he releases me from the hug, I feel his sweat clinging to me, my arms and shirt damp.

"I haven't seen you in forever, girl."

"I know. I've been busy with school, and my dad doesn't make it out here much."

He pats me on the head, his hand covering my hair like a hat, and I remember the way we played when I was younger. My father would be busy talking with Coach Turner, parsing out things before practice, and Freeman would keep an eye on me. Most times, he'd teach me things about being a defensive tackle. He'd get down on his knees, have me drop to a three-point stance, and he'd let me try to swim past his blocks. I remember trying to run around him only to find his huge form shuffling into my path, his arms roping out to stop me.

"You played good last week," I say, and he thanks me, though we both know that he's having a harder time getting through the line these days. The techniques he taught me don't work as well anymore, not with his knees gone out.

"I got to pop in to see Coach in a minute. Want to help get this tape off?" he says.

"Sure." I follow him to a couple of chairs outside Coach Turner's office, and I begin to unwrap the tape on his wrists. When I was six, I taped and untaped my father's ankles and wrists. There was a ritual to it, pre- and post-game. Now, the tape sticking to my hands, I realize that this may be the last time I do this. A final unwinding.

Once I'm done with his wrists, Freeman props his foot up, and I begin to unwrap his ankle.

"Why's Redbarn getting traded?" I ask.

Freeman is looking at his ankles, at my hands unwinding the tape, its thick layers of protection for his joints. I un-loop it from around the ankle twice, then from around his foot, then back to the ankle again, repeating the process.

"I don't know. Best for the team, I guess."

"Is he here?"

"Supposed to be here for practice yesterday, but he didn't show. I don't know much more than you do, Wilma."

I switch to his other foot, begin to work on it.

"Thanks, girl. Getting to be a pain doing this myself."

When I've removed the last of it, he stands, and I notice that sitting, I barely reach his waist.

"Good luck this week."

"Luck ain't got nothing to do with it . . ."

I smile. "Skill and planning's all you need," I say, finishing my father's standard line.

"Come by more often." He walks into Coach Turner's office, and I think for a moment about following him, but instead, I get up and move away, back down the hallway.

I know why Freeman doesn't want to talk about these things. I understand why someone like Freeman can't focus on Redbarn being traded. He's getting older, his abilities are declining. The team could decide to squeeze some value from Freeman, see if they can pick up a couple of late-round picks for him. Or they might decide his contract isn't worth paying and cut him. It's better to think of the moment. The next game. The next practice. The next play.

———

The next day, I'm sitting on a bench at the park in Deer Valley, facing a big, grassy field. I'm running Kevin through drills from where I sit. The expanse of grass we're on is bigger than the Chiefs' practice field, and it's mostly empty. A group of runners make their way around a track off to our right. A few people walk dogs, but beyond that, it's just the two of us.

Kevin's jogging in place until I clap my hands. I wish that I had a whistle, like Coach Turner wears. I should get one, should ask my father. He's surely got one in the house somewhere, but whether he remembers where is an issue.

Each time I clap, Kevin drops to the ground, pushes himself back up, and resumes jogging. It's a tiring exercise, but it works his core.

"Nobody's going to say anything to me about Redbarn," I say. Kevin is facing forward, his head bobbing as he jogs. I clap, and he drops, pushes off the ground.

"Maybe they don't know anything," he says, his breath coming in quick bursts. I clap my hands again.

"What do you mean?" I ask.

He's back on his feet, slower this time. I think this is good for him, this is what training is for. "Maybe it's just one of those decisions a team makes." The words come slow, one at a time between chugs of air. I clap twice, telling him that he can stop. He drops to the ground.

I look out across the field, to the jogging path. Among the runners, I see a familiar stoop-shouldered lope. Before Kevin can stop me, I'm up and away, rushing across the open field, to the track. By the time I get there, I'm well behind him, with lots of other joggers between us. As I push myself forward, move through these people, I briefly imagine myself a running back, juking and weaving my way through holes my offensive line is opening. It takes me a minute to catch up, to get to Patrick Rhoda, general manager of the Chiefs.

Kevin is beside me. He's breathing hard, and for a minute, I let myself feel proud that he was able to catch up to me even after the workout I've put him through.

Rhoda is tall and angular, like a wideout, but he moves in a perpetual hunch, as if apologizing constantly for his height. He's moving forward in long strides, covering the distance quickly, and I'm pushing myself to keep up.

"Mr. Rhoda," I say, breathing hard.

He turns his head, recognizes me, smiles.

"Mr. Rhoda," I say, again. "I wanted to ask about Redbarn."

He shakes his head, says, "Got to finish my run." I can't tell if he even heard what I said over his puffing and wheezing.

"I just have a question."

"Have a good one!" He puts on a burst of speed, moving away from us, and I let myself wish that I had the size of Freeman or of my father. I picture this man trying to outrun my father at his prime. I imagine my dad's long arms snaking out from behind him, pulling him down, the way he did with so many running backs through the years. I imagine standing over him, asking him all the questions I want to ask.

I slow to a trot and realize that Kevin's still right beside me. "You can't do that," he says.

"I wanted to ask about Redbarn."

Kevin shakes his head. He moves off the track, to an open bench.

"I just wanted to know," I say, but the words sound weak now. I think of my father, his nose broken and bloodied at halftime of a meaningless late season game against the Oilers, pulling his helmet back on, getting ready to go back on the field. I went down to field level, held his helmet and a towel for him while the trainers pulled his nose down until the bone that had bulged to the top formed something closer to a straight line. Blood had come out in bubbling spurts, and I'd looked away, afraid that he would lose too much of it.

Kevin motions again, and I sit. "They aren't going to talk about it with you."

I shake my head. "Someone knows why they'd trade him. People care."

He looks at me, but he doesn't say anything, and I can see the truth in his eyes. Redbarn is a minor defensive player in a league stacked with all-stars. The people who have noticed are more worried about the logistics of the trade than they are about what will become of Redbarn on some other team, whether another organization will value him, whether he'll live up to the potential I've always seen in him. In a week, they'll forget him completely, but I won't.

I look at Kevin. "You know you'll never be that good."

He looks back at me, confused.

"You're never going to play in the NFL. You won't even play college ball. I'm busting my ass to get you on the varsity team at a private school that sends one kid every decade to play at the next level."

"I don't—" he begins.

"You will never be a football player. You're weak, and you're slow. You don't have the instinct for it."

He stares at me, mouth open.

"I should have told you this a long time ago," I say, and I turn from him. As I walk across the field to the parking lot, to my father's car, I wait for the touch of his hand on my shoulder, but it doesn't come.

———

It's late when I get back to the house, and my father's already sleeping. He's still in his chair, but his head has dropped to the surface of the desk. I shake him awake and guide him to his room. He's only half-aware, and as I cover him with his old blanket, he thanks me, the way I used to hear him thank refs on a good call. I wonder briefly if he made it down to the kitchen today, if he got anything to eat.

I go back to his study, sit at the desk. I pick up his chalkboard, swipe my sleeve across it until everything he's drawn is wiped away. I hold the chalk, begin to draw a new formation, but it's random, positions clustered, arrows indicating blitzes and routes mingling in a way they shouldn't. I should know how to do this. I should be good at this, like my father is, even in this state.

After a moment, I stand up and walk to the front door. I grab his keys and head out into the night.

The streets are mostly deserted. I cruise slowly to the football complex, where the guards wave me in. I leave the car in the player parking area. In the front offices, the lights in the hall are half off, and I notice that in the lower light I can see more of the cracks and creases in the walls. Something about the brightness of the daytime washes it out, makes those walls look smooth, sculpted, but now, with pools of shadow and yellow half-light, I can see decay in the place.

It takes me a few minutes of winding through the hallways before I find myself in front of the big double doors. Coach Turner gave my father the key years ago, so that he could come and work out whenever he wanted to. I slip through the doors and out into the night air of the practice field. It's dark out here, set off from the lights at the front of the building, the streetlights, and the glow of businesses. The building shields it, and as I walk toward the middle of the field, I imagine the world outside this field, outside of our neighborhood. These are the only worlds I've known for more than a decade.

When I was seven, I failed a math test, an important one. My mother came up from Mississippi, and she yelled at me and my father for a while. She said I focused too much on football. At one point, she asked what I thought I'd do with myself if I kept failing tests. I remember the way my father's face fell. At the time, I didn't understand his reaction.

I looked my mother in the eye and said, "I'm going to play football."

She laughed for a long time, then yelled more, and finally left, going back to her own home, to her new husband and my brother, who was still too young to understand anything that had happened. When it was just me and my father, both of us sitting on the edge of my bed, he reached over and put a hand on my back to stop me from crying.

"Let's go out to the field," he said.

It was the first time I'd been there when it was empty. The lights high on their poles were off, so when my father let the door swing closed behind us, the field was in perfect darkness. Now, I remember the feel of the grass under my feet. I remember the way my shoes sank down in it a little. It seemed so soft. My father, one hand on my back, guided me out onto the field. When we were near what must have been midfield, he asked me if my eyes were open. I told him they weren't. "Why not?" he said.

I opened my eyes. "I can't see anything."

"So why should your eyes be closed?"

"I don't know," I said.

"Keep them open."

"OK."

He took his hand off my back. "I want you to look at the trees, off there in the distance."

"I can't see them."

"OK," he said. "I want you to look at the moon."

"It's not there tonight."

"Look at the ground."

"I can kind of see my feet."

"So you can't see much. What do you hear?"

"You. Talking."

He laughed. "When I'm not talking, what do you hear?"

I let the echo of his words fade, and I listened, but there was nothing. There was no hum of the big lights, no buzz of crickets, no bustle of other people. "I can't hear anything."

"Good. Standing there, what do you feel?"

"The ground, I guess."

"OK, you feel the ground. What's it feel like?"

I concentrated on the way my feet sank down into the grass. "Soft, like it shouldn't be holding me up, but it is."

"Most people don't think about the grass. They worry about their assignments, about the play, about what the other team's going to do, but they don't think about the simplest part of the game. Your feet. The grass. It makes everything else possible."

I realized in that moment that I couldn't imagine my mother in this world, couldn't imagine her anywhere but where she was now. They'd been married five years before I was born. She'd been the loyal trophy wife, on the sidelines for every game, but I couldn't imagine my father telling her these things. Couldn't imagine her receiving them.

"Wilma," he said, "ask me a question about the world." I heard him move away, off to the side somewhere.

"What kind of question?"

"Any kind."

The darkness of the field felt unending, and maybe that's what prompted me to ask the cliché kid question: why is the sky the way it is? I didn't understand how it worked, how something could just go on and on, without any edge.

He didn't laugh. From the darkness off to the side, he said, "Sometimes there's too much to know about the world. It's good to want to know how things work, but don't try to understand everything. Find something you can know and focus on that."

"Is that what you do?"

"I focus on football."

How could he stop wanting to know about everything else?

He continued, "When you're looking out at the sky, when you see an animal doing something unimaginable, when you want to know how a plant grows, filter it through football. Don't try to imagine the world. Try to imagine football."

At the time, I didn't understand what he wanted me to do, what those words meant, so I stood on that dark field with my eyes open. My mind kept shifting back to my mother, focusing on the way she'd laughed at me. After a time, he came back, told me it was time to go. We didn't talk as we left the field, the building, as we got in the car and drove back home. It wasn't until we were in the driveway that he said, "There's plenty to worry with in the world without forgetting what matters to you most."

Now, I try to recreate those few minutes in the dark. On this field again, there is nothing but the silence of the world. There is only the feel of soft grass under my feet.

A quick shaft of light slants onto the field as the door opens and closes behind me. By the time I've turned around, the door is closed again, and I can't see anything.

After a moment, a bank of lights above me flash on with an electric hum, and I see Coach Turner, standing off to one side.

He doesn't seem surprised to see me. "Wilma."

"Coach."

He walks over, slowly. "Jimmy know you're here?"

"I used his key. I'm sorry."

"It's okay. How's he doing?"

"Working on plays."

He nods, and I know that he's wondering the same thing as me. When will they stop pretending? When will Turner stop being able to justify my dad's presence to the front office suits?

"I have a question, Coach."

He reaches out, pats me on the shoulder. "You should probably get going."

"What happened with Redbarn?"

His face is turned away from me, half lost in the shadows, but when he talks, I can hear the strain in his voice. "Wilma, we make a lot of hard decisions in this business."

"Why him?"

"It's what's best for the team," he says. I've heard this tone of voice before, when he tells players to stop asking for playing time or to run another ten laps or to hit the sleds once more. There isn't an inch left between the words for discussion.

"I was just curious," I say, and though I don't want to admit it, I'm hurt that he's used this voice on me, that he's treating me the way he treats everyone else. I think of my father going down on the field that last time, of the trainers loading him onto the stretcher, of the cart that took him from the field, into the locker room, and from there out to an ambulance. When it was over, Coach Turner lied, told them that my father had been drawing up schemes and formations for him all along. We all knew he couldn't play anymore, but we didn't know then how bad it would get.

Coach Turner looks at me, and in this dim half-light, I notice for the first time how the skin under his eyes has softened, begun to sag. He's been coaching for as long as I've been alive, longer. In my mind, I see him at the White House, standing next to my father, both smiling, watching me as I explored. They'd won the Super Bowl that year, when I was four. I got to come along. I don't remember it at all, but my father has told me about it enough times that it feels real. I know that I shouldn't, but I say, "Redbarn was hurt, wasn't he?"

Coach Turner's eyes narrow, and his hand drops on my shoulder. He gives me the briefest of nods, just a tilt of the head. "Tell your father I said hi. Tell him that I'm looking forward to seeing those new plays."

He begins walking, his hand still on my shoulder, and I move with him, toward the door.

———

Back in the study at home, I sit down at the desk. While I was gone, my father got up from bed, came back to his chalkboard. He's erased half of my scribbles, pared down the drawing to focus on a blitz I didn't realize I was building. He's shifted the defensive end's assignment, pulled a safety into the box, but my arrow for the Mike is still there, still pointing through the line, and around it, he's drawn a circle, for emphasis. He is asleep on the couch in the corner now, and I listen to him snoring softly, a little wheeze of breath.

I think about waking my father, asking him if this play could be good, if he'll leave the other safety high, if the corners will be in man or zone. Instead, I switch off the light and stumble through the dark out to the hallway, to my room, to my bed.

I remember being five, my father trying to explain why my mother didn't stay with us in our house anymore, how she wanted to be closer to family in Mississippi, how this was better for everyone. At six, he tried to explain why I needed to focus during school, and at seven, he told me to close my eyes and feel the grass underneath my feet.

Now, lying on my bed in the dark, I think of Redbarn and of Coach Turner and of my father, and I tell myself that I can't ask more questions. Everything about my life now urges me to forget. I can't think about what the game did to my father or about Redbarn's injury. I can't confront these things too directly. All I can do now is move forward. Still, for a moment I remember the way my father played, how he could swim past a tight end on his way to sack the quarterback. How, when he dropped back into coverage, his backpedal was so smooth it looked like he wasn't going backward at all. I reach up to the wall, feel the carved names. For the first time, I think of the possible meanings behind my crush on Redbarn. I think of my father and Redbarn on the field at the same time. They could have anchored a legendary defense, I tell myself. My father could have gotten the best out of Redbarn, could have gotten plays out of him that he can't get out of himself. One thing my father has taught me is that sometimes success depends on what the other players on the field are doing. Sometimes, it's less about where you are on the field than it is about where your teammates are. On the field together, my father could have created mismatches with the offense that would have helped Redbarn live up to his potential. I want to believe that in the end, the game can be something good.

Tomorrow, I will scratch the names out. Tomorrow, I'll apologize to Kevin by teaching him how to juke a defender. I'll make sure my father eats. I'll bury myself in those actions, my focus narrowed to this world around me, though lying here now, my fingers grazing the carved names, I imagine a knife in my hand, the blade scratching the walls, bit by bit, beginning with the divoted letters and moving deeper, the blade chipping and breaking through the hard brick. I imagine pushing free of this house, out into the yard that surrounds us, soft after the hard resistance of this wall, but as I lie in the grass, the blade doesn't stop moving, it shovels out dirt. I can smell the stench of earth, can feel the grit of it, but my hand keeps moving, the blade angling deeper, working at the ground until it pushes free into the open air, my arm tickled by the grass, my hand deep in the hole I've dug. I concentrate on the rough letters, imagine the knife. In my mind, I climb down from the grassy yard, a night wind bristling at my arms as I lower myself into the hole. The sky above me is so, so simple.

The Other Dog

They slept. It had been a long day hiking, up and over and through, and so when they, the father and the daughter, made camp at the edge of the Ouiska Chitto Creek and cooked a can of beans to share and drank each from the bottle of Four Roses the father carried in his pack, they tucked into their sleeping bags and curled against the cool late evening, still not even fully night, and slept.

When they woke in the morning, it was to the sound of barking. The daughter rose first, hearing the call and response of two dogs in the tangle of woods at their back. She rose from her sleeping bag and looked across the misty creek. The bank spread out around their little camp for fifty feet before it gave way to the thick trees she and her father had come through the previous day. She stretched, lifted her leg to ease the morning cramp in her calf. "Dad," she said, as the dogs barked again. It wasn't an angry bark, not a warning to some animal. It was the holler of two dogs at play, and it made her smile, thinking of these animals here in the wilderness, finding joy in each other's company. "Dad," she said again, and finally he stirred, rose bleary from his sleeping bag.

They'd brought biscuits wrapped in wax paper, which they ate cold, with strips of fresh beef jerky. They'd brought no coffee, so they washed the food down with water from their canteens and a quick swig of the bourbon to fortify them for the day. All through their breakfast, they heard the dogs, and the daughter thought of her father's favorite dog, a golden retriever he'd gotten when she was in kindergarten. He'd brought the dog, still a small puppy, to her school when he picked her up that day, and she remembered the way it made her feel to have all her friends and her teachers want to hold and pet the puppy. They'd had the dog all through her childhood, but it died the summer before she left for college, and in the years since, her father had not been able to bring himself to get a new one.

"I figured we'd follow the creek for a bit today," the father said.

"Sounds good to me."

They were rolling their sleeping bags and preparing to move out when the dogs emerged from the woods. The daughter had expected them to be disparately sized based on the two different barks, one a deep, bellowing woof, the other a chirping trill, but they looked like siblings, two midsized mutts with similar black and tan markings and high, pointed ears that stood up straight as they bounded onto the banks of the creek.

The father and the daughter, in unison, began to call to them, to coo and baby-talk them closer, and the dogs did not hesitate. They came eagerly, allowed the father and the daughter to pet them, to feed them each a strip of jerky, and to examine their tags, which identified them as Pancho and Lefty, a joke the father found amusing. Each tag was etched with the same local telephone number.

"We should bring them with us," the daughter said. "They must have gotten out. I bet their owner's worried sick."

"How'd they get this deep in the woods?" the father said. He was scratching Lefty behind the ears, and the dog panted appreciatively.

"OK, you two," the girl said, lifting her pack. "Y'all are coming with us."

They walked for a long hour along the bank of the creek. At times, the sandy expanse shriveled and shrank, and they had to walk through ankle-deep water or else weave in and out of the trees at the edge of the woods. The dogs trotted with them, stopping now and again to drink greedily from the slow-moving water. They'd fallen into a rhythm, the four of them, and the daughter began to wonder about keeping them, about what they could do with these two dogs (who already felt like their own) if the owner didn't want them, if they hadn't gotten out by mistake but had instead been let out purposefully. She fantasized briefly about going to the owner's home and discovering that the dogs were being mistreated. She thought about the righteous indignation she would level at the man if she discovered this, but she shook herself from this reverie and felt immediately guilty for it, wishing harm on these dogs so that she'd have a reason to keep them. Still, as they walked, she would reach down occasionally and trail her fingers along the dogs' bristly fur and feel a rightness to the match. It felt like fate, the dogs finding them there and joining them so readily. It was a squirrel that broke the peace.

They'd reached a bend in the creek, the kind of jogging shift the father always called a dogleg. The daughter was looking at the water. The father was looking at the sky. Neither saw the squirrel bolt out into the clearing, but Pancho saw it, and he leapt from beside them, darted out across the sand and into the tangle of woods without stopping. Lefty sat beside the daughter, scratched behind his ear.

"We have to go after him," the daughter said. She called the dog's name, trying to be loud without sounding frightened, trying to bellow so that her voice would carry.

"Into the woods?" the father said. "He might come back on his own." He, too, called out for Pancho.

The daughter dropped to a crouch, fumbled in her bag until she came out with a length of knotted rope. When she was a child, the father had endlessly cataloged the necessities of hiking for her. He had been meticulous about it. Now, the daughter always carried a length of rope, a good knife, water purification tablets, a first aid kit, and a handful of other odds and ends.

She unwound the rope, held Lefty by the collar, and led him to the edge of the clearing, where a river oak had fallen. She tied one end of the rope to Lefty's collar and the other securely to a thick, sturdy branch.

Lefty whined. She patted his head, told him he was a good boy, that they'd be back. She thought, briefly, that maybe they should bring him with them, but then she thought of the brambles and knotting vines they may have to go through to get to Pancho, and she decided it would be better for him here, safe by the creek. The father and the daughter walked into the woods.

———

There was no path for the daughter and the father to adhere to. The father would have liked to have had one, a stretch of cleared brush, even a narrow one, that they could use as a landmark for their searching. Instead, they tumbled through underbrush, freed themselves from tangled vines and the grabbing branches of small trees. They moved through all of this slowly, methodically, calling out to Pancho as they pushed in the general direction they believed he'd gone.

"He couldn't have gotten far in all of this," the daughter said, but the father wasn't so sure.

The day was warming gradually. Above them in the canopy of trees, they heard the chatter and singing of birds at play. The daughter looked up and thought briefly of her mother. Many years ago, she'd come with them, had brought her thick *Guide to North American Birds*, and had tutored the daughter on birdwatching, though now, these years later, her mother gone, she looked at the grouping of birds, coming together and breaking apart in the shadowy tree cover, and she said quietly, "A murmuration."

In the distance, the daughter thought she could hear the scuffling of the dog, but she realized it could be anything making that noise. She looked at her father. He wiped at his forehead, where a branch or bramble had nicked him, smearing the blood as though it were sweat. He smiled when he realized she was watching him, said, "Just another father-daughter adventure," in a faux-cheerful voice.

The daughter smiled back, though the deeper they moved into the woods, the more guilt she felt for insisting they go after the dog. This was not how their hikes were supposed to go. She was about to suggest they turn and go back when the tangle of trees lightened, space opened up between them, and they found themselves emerging into a small clearing.

Though the grass grew tall here, tangled with vines and weeds, there were no trees, and at the center of the open space was a little house of rough wood, long abandoned. The corner of the roof sloped low, beaten down from the years, and the windows were smudged with grime. The front door stood open, and from inside, they could hear the dog scuffling, rooting.

At the doorway, the father called out, "Hello?" He turned to the daughter. "Just in case someone actually lives here." There was no response, and the daughter crossed the threshold.

Dust layered the sparse room they walked into. An old table and chair were coated. A tipped coatrack lay on the floor, its top gray from the dust, its bottom still the rich brown of its wood. The only disruption to the blanket of dust was the dog's footprints, which ran the length of the room. "Pancho," the daughter called quietly. She did not know why she was being quiet or why she was moving through the room slowly, with a kind of reverence, but she found herself trailing a slow finger across the tabletop, the near wall, as she moved to the little hallway.

The father found Pancho. In the back room, next to an old metal-frame bed, a hole was broken out from the floorboards, and in the dark of the narrow crawl space below, the father could see the dog's nose peeking into a small band of light. "Hey, buddy," the father said, dropping beside the hole. "I found him."

The daughter came into the room, knowing immediately that something was wrong. "Is he okay?"

"Oh, sure," the father said. "We just need to get him out of this hole." He reached a hand down to coax the dog forward, closer to the hole where he could reach down and lift him out, but the dog backed away, retreated into the crawl space.

"Let me try," the daughter said. She took off her backpack and brought out the jerky. Dangling a piece above the hole, she called the dog's name, spoke it with the same soothing whisper her mother had used when waking her for school each morning. She repeated the dog's name over and over, wishing she could run a hand along his head, could ease him out with her words and with the physical connection, as well.

"I don't think he's coming out," the father said. He stood, hands on hips. Many years before, his wife had called it his "engineer pose." A tree fallen across the shed after a hurricane would lead to twenty minutes of the father standing in the yard, hands on hips, surveying and planning before moving to act. After a time, the father said, "Slide back."

He dropped to the floor where the daughter had been, braced his hands against one of the floorboards, and began to pull. The wood was old, untreated, and disintegrating, and the nails pulled free quickly. The father tugged upward until the board was prized free. The hole, larger now, revealed the edge of the dog. His head was still in shadow, but they could see his right side, and with this new view, they began to understand.

The dog's hind leg was swelling. On the haunch, two bright red puncture wounds oozed pink. "Snakebite," the daughter said, and the father nodded.

The daughter began to tug more floorboards loose. The dog whined. "It's alright, buddy," the father said. "It's okay."

When the hole was large enough to reveal the whole dog, the daughter dropped in over her father's warning. She reached down to the dog and lifted him gently. She had expected him to snap at her out of defensiveness, but he eyed her sadly, whined briefly, and acquiesced.

The father took him from her and laid him on the floor while she climbed from the hole. "Should we try to suck the venom?" the daughter said.

"It's too late for that," the father said, eyeing the inflammation.

"What do we do?"

The father did not answer at first. His mind uncoiled, the memory of a cold February morning rising up. He'd stood in a chilly falling rain, phone in hand, trying to get the courage to call the daughter, to tell her that it was over, that her mother was gone. He was soaked by the time he made the phone call, and he remembered still the feel of the warm bath he drew, the way he tried without success to leach the shivering from his body. "We can't do anything for him," the father said. "Maybe make him comfortable."

Tears rolled down the daughter's cheeks and dropped heavy to the dusty floor.

"Let's get him on the bed," the father said, not knowing why he hadn't laid him there to begin with. Together they lifted him from the floor and laid him down.

"We should give him some water," the daughter said. She took her canteen out, uncapped it, dribbled water on the dog's nose, but he didn't lap at it, just shifted his head away. "Drink, buddy," she said, trying again, but the dog would not drink, and so she capped the canteen and put it away.

The father felt the length of the dog's body. Ran his hands up the fur, ruffling it, and then again in the other direction, smoothing it down. He wondered if it would be better to rub hard, to massage the dog and soothe his pain, or if a light touch were needed. The daughter thought of adding her hands to the rubbing, but she did not.

They looked at the dog, and each of them in their turn tried not to think of the daughter's mother and the father's wife, lying sick, but they each failed, memories of her coming in the way they always did.

"Pancho," the daughter said, after a time. The father rested his hand on the dog's head. "Pancho," she said again, and as she spoke his name, the dog breathed one final breath and died.

The daughter and the father walked their long path back to the banks of the Ouiska Chitto Creek without speaking. The daughter thought of asking the father questions, the kind she would have asked as a little girl. She thought of holding onto him, crying into his shirt and asking, "But why?" Instead, they walked in the quiet of the late morning, passing between them the bottle of Four Roses.

All around them the trees shushed with a low wind, their leaves speaking the news of the world, but the birds had all gone, and they saw no deer or squirrels or other animals.

They came back to the sandy shoreline and found Lefty, who sat panting and scratching, a grin spread across his face. The daughter went to him and untied the length of rope. He trotted around, pissed in the sand, barked once.

The father thought of how to tell the dog that his brother was gone. He dropped down beside the other dog and ran his hands along the dog's back, ruffling the fur the way his own dog, his now-dead retriever, had liked. The daughter dropped beside him too. She scratched beneath his chin and lifted his head to look into his eyes, which were either happy or baleful.

The father and the daughter sat with Lefty a long while, thinking of what could be done, but when they finally came to understand that there was nothing left but to walk away from the Ouiska Chitto and out of the woods, they stood and tightened their packs and tied the length of rope around the other dog's collar to lead him back.

Five Star

When the guy hands you the grocery sack full of cash, you realize that maybe you shouldn't have come after all. For most of your life the days have stretched out at an achingly slow pace, kindergarten ceding to high school so gradually that you'd swear you were near middle age by the time you hit freshman year. Your mother didn't make things any better with her OK-but-don't nagging. Want to go to a sleepover? OK but don't stay up too late. Signing up for an advanced class? OK but don't overload on those classes, you're still a young man. Signing up for football? OK but don't think you have to live up to your father's exploits, you'll just hurt yourself, I don't want to see anything bad happen to you.

That last one, the decision to go out for the team three years ago, is the one that kicked your life into overdrive, the one that sent freshmansophomorejunior years careening past and placed you here, in this parking lot, three days before the last game of your senior year, with a sackful of twenties crumpled in your fist and a dude in a sport coat grinning at you expectantly.

———

They say you've got hips. That's what you've read about yourself on the recruiting services, on the message boards, in the comment threads of all the state's newspapers. "Kid's got hips." "Quick twitch. Look at those hips." "We need a corner with hips like that." You've read these things about yourself, printed them out and shown them to your mother, who clucks her tongue and tells you not to get a big head, not to turn your nose up quite so high, but you can still see a nub of excitement elbowing its way through her disapproval.

"I'll handle your recruitment," she said, and you agreed, let her field the calls and organize the letters from schools. When the reporters started reaching out, it was her who told them that you wouldn't be committing until after your senior season, that you'd make your announcement at the All-America game (sponsored by Clothing Apparel Brand A) to which you've only just received an invitation, and not at the other All-America game (sponsored by Clothing Apparel Brand B and a branch of the US military).

Your coach resisted this arrangement at first, telling her that he was the one with experience in such matters. He is not, of course. None of you have experience with these things. Your coach has never had a player of your caliber, and for all his moralizing and hand-wringing—he has a morality agreement you've had to sign each fall before the season begins that stipulates no sex, no alcohol, no drugs, no violence—you wonder how he'd respond to you, his star player, breaking that agreement in a big, blatant way. It's better that your mother is handling all of this. If things turn south, if your conversation with Tina tonight doesn't go well, at least *she'll* still try to do what's best for you.

To her credit, she *has* tried to shelter you from the buzz. It seeps in at the edges at school, though, and when your teammates show you the pages—the ones that you print off to show her in turn—you can feel the minutes ticking off the clock a little faster, can feel that second hand whir.

———

It's not just the recruitment that does it. You've felt this way since you set foot on the field. Aside from backyard games with your friends, you'd never played organized ball, but in the opening practice, the coaches recognized your speed. They tried you at receiver first, but your hands, let's be honest, aren't what they need to be, and even in ninth grade you were over six foot two, plenty tall enough to play corner in your school's division. It didn't take you long to pick up the basics, especially since the defensive coaches were smart enough to say, "Line up on your man and don't let him catch the ball." When you slip into a backpedal, shift your hips—*those hips!* they say—and break on a route, the clock speeds up and it's like you're not even alive anymore, like the whole thing is just over and done with. One of the articles called your play "effortless," and you don't know if that's entirely correct—you work as hard as anyone else—but it isn't entirely incorrect either. There's a moment when you slip back into coverage when it really *is* effortless, when the world recedes from your vision and you can glide on over to the guy trying to catch the ball, when you can hop right up in front of him and pluck that ball yourself, or failing that—*his hands*, they say, *if only his hands were better*—swat the thing to the turf, and the whistle blows, and *dingdingding*, everyone's back there around you again until the next snap, when you can glide on back again and let the noise fade.

———

The guy's looking at you expectantly still, and you realize you've zoned out a little bit, that you've *lost track of time*, which is the phrase you use with your mother when you miss curfew these days. "So, what do you think?" he says.

"Sounds great," you say, though you're not sure exactly what he's talking about. He breaks into a smile, though, and you stick out your hand to shake, figuring that this is the best way to speed along the whole process. You need the money in the bag. Without the money in the bag, all of this could go away, all of this could be swept away, and your life could go back to the *tick-tock-tick* of orderliness and routine. Without the money, you won't even have Tina anymore. With the money, you might still not have her anymore. There's that conversation waiting to be had, waiting for when you're done here, and that conversation could go in any direction Tina chooses once you've said what you're going to say.

The dude shakes your hand back, still grinning, and you wonder if you just unintentionally committed to his school.

———

You met Tina at a party you weren't supposed to be at, one that got you in trouble with your mother, who said, "You're too smart for all of this," and she's kind of right, you are really smart, and you know better than to do the things you do, but when has that ever stopped anyone before? Napoleon was smart as hell—infantry square, anyone?—but look at the dumb shit he did that ended up tanking his whole deal. When you allow yourself to really think about it, Tina might as well have been named Water L. Oo instead of Tina Grace Lewis. You slid up to her at that party, dipped your hand into the hip pocket of her jeans, and she reared back and hit you—not slapped, never slapped with Tina, only full-on balled fist hit—and when you'd shaken loose the hit-induced cobwebs, she'd told you not to fuck with her, that she has brothers who taught her to punch, and that she'd be happy to knock the shit out of you again if you ever decided to put your hands on her. Your mother would dislike her on principle—she's a girl, and girls are distractions—but you know that at her core, Tina is exactly the kind of girl your mother would want to raise. You apologized, and it took time—four more parties' worth of time!—but eventually *she* sidled up to *you* in the hallway between classes, slid *her* hand into *your* pocket, and green light go, that was all it took to tumble time along and leave you standing here with this guy and this money.

——

"You got a few minutes?" the guy says, and you think briefly of Tina, sitting in her bedroom, not knowing that she's waiting on your arrival. You can delay that a few minutes, though, can push back *that* particular conversation, so you nod your head to the dude. His car is all leather and the kind of spit-shine clean that means he pays for detailing, like, all the time. He just sits a minute, and you worry that he might reach over and touch your leg or something, but he turns the key, revs the engine, jerks out of the parking lot and onto Highway 85.

He drives fast, turning that German engine loose, and you wonder if he'll let you drive it. You're pretty sure he would, pretty sure he'd hand over the keys and tell you to keep the whole damn car if you asked, but that's the kind of thing people notice, the kind of thing that could shut down your forward progress, stall you right out and back into the slow trudge of everything that came before your *gift* asserted itself, and anyway, all of this is about keeping yourself under the radar, about maintaining the direction of your life.

Value, the old saying goes, is intrinsic. Yes, indeed, and your value means that you have power. The ability to make decisions—to ask for the car or not, to take the cash or not, to commit to the old guy's team or not—is power, and power means not slowing down. You've never seen a sports car sit idling on the side of the road. *Move*, you think, and the guy, foot heavy on the pedal, obliges.

——

Tina likes talking, and you like this about her. She talks when you pick her up in your mother's Corolla, talks through dinner at the Mexican restaurant where you always take her, whispers in your ear the name of every actor in every movie—lists full damn filmographies in her gravel-husk whisper, enough to get you wrought-iron hard. She talks as you go down on her, pauses her blowjobs to talk, talks between gulps of air as she comes. She talks about *everything*, her family—three older brothers, dead mother, remarried father, icy stepmother ("Like, *brrrr*, seriously, you get me?"). Her schoolwork and her teachers and her friends, the car she wants, the cars she doesn't want, her lunches and breakfasts and the M&M's she stole from some kid's backpack, books ("Only book worth burning is shitty-ass *Fahrenheit 451*") and TV, the gender-restrictive rules that keep her from taking off her top at the beach ("You got tits too, motherfucker, but they ain't as nice as mine"), energy-efficient lightbulbs, the way that paint dries. All the things of the world come tumbling out of her mouth, and you listen and nod and sometimes say something back, trying not to sound too oblivious to the ideas she's spouting, but mostly you just listen because she gets you *going* with all that talk, revs *your* engine, and when you're inside her and she's meandering through a discussion of the value of sensible gun control, you don't feel anything at all but the thrust and the clench that accompanies it, and that clench, that holding at peak thrust, is enough to make you do pretty much anything to keep feeling that thrust-clinch, thrust-clench, thrust-clench, with the soundtrack of her talking smothering every other last thing, even the knowledge that all of this is temporary, that in another month she won't be able to hide the pooch, won't be able to pretend to her father or brothers that she isn't preggers, knocked up, bun-in-ovened, with child.

———

The guy stops in a pawn shop parking lot next door to the public library. You went there often as a boy, your mother dropping you off for long stretches of your summer. You'd roam the stacks without supervision, reading what caught your eye. Those were the days before they had computers, so you had no distractions, and though you haven't set foot in the place in years, you feel a pang of nostalgia that's tempered with the ever-present desire to run, to get away, to escape from the familiar.

The parking lot of the pawn shop is empty but for the guy's car. You look over, across the little expanse of grass that separates the two buildings, and the library looks like a cave, vast and dark. Its big plate-glass doors reveal nothing of the building's interior.

"Know where we are?" the guy says.

"A pawn shop. And that's the library," you say, wanting suddenly to tell him more, to explain your history with that place, though you keep quiet, wait for him to respond.

"Jimmy's Pawn and Gun." He drums his fingers on the steering wheel. "Know who Jimmy was?"

You shake your head. It's getting hot in the car, and you can feel that warmth rising from the leather seats. The realization that they're heated thunders up on you unbidden. It's a strange realization. Why wouldn't these seats be heated? Of course they are. This should not be shocking, but you find yourself shaken, not so much by the knowledge itself as by the fact that this luxury is *uncomfortable*. You are too warm in here, too cushioned by this gentle heat. A bead of sweat rolls down from your underarm, tickling your side beneath the workout jersey you still wear.

"Jimmy Profford played for us near fifty years ago. He was a fullback. An All-American. Got his business degree, got money, opened these shops." He nudges his chin toward the little pawn shop. "Got that building there paid outright when he was thirty. Got five other locations scattered across this part of the state. One of them in Wyeth, right near campus. When you get to campus, you're gonna live in a building he helped pay to build. Finest athletics dorm you'll find. Latest amenities."

"OK," you say, after a time.

"Son," he says, turning to face you, "you apply yourself with us and sky's the damn limit. You can be anything you want to be." He laughs, shakes his head. "And if you wanna shut down LSU's receivers for a few years while you do it, we'd be real happy about that."

"Yes, sir," you say.

He clucks his tongue, looks at the dark building a while longer. "Jimmy Profford was my father. This is my store now. Not the one I manage day-to-day, mind you. That's the one in Wyeth. But this one's mine too." He turns to you. "You ready?" he says, and you say that you are, that he can take you back to your car now.

Here is what your mother would say if she knew about Tina: I can't believe you. I let you play a game, let you do what you want to do, and this is what I get in return? You're a cliché. The football star and his knocked-up girlfriend. You've made yourself typical, do you know that? That you are average now? That you're just another one of *them*? You have a family now, and *my* son is going to do the thing I raised him to do. Playtime is over.

You are three blocks from the parking lot where your car waits for you when the dude goes, "You ain't got a father, do you?"

You tell him that you had a father. That he is dead now, but before you've even finished your sentence, he is saying that a boy needs a man in his life, needs a mentor and a father figure, or he'll never amount to anything.

You tell him that your mother has raised you right, that your coach takes care of you, too, though this isn't exactly true. Your coach cares about you only inasmuch as you can score him a better coaching gig. The dream—his dream—is to jump to college, and your name on his résumé could make that happen for him, if he's willing to grind it out at a smaller school as a position coach for a few years. But who are you kidding? He's willing. He's ready to do this, to springboard his ass right out of this city and into a better place. That you happen to be the board from which he'll be springing doesn't bother you particularly. No, it doesn't bother you. You find it . . . amusing? Yes. You find his inability to shape his own destiny to be amusing. A little sad, maybe, but mostly amusing, and so you let him squeeze your shoulder after games, when the cameras are rolling. You let him talk about pride and desire and ability.

The old guy is rambling on about the necessity for a defining force in life, and you're pretty sure he got this whole spiel from a self-help book, but you don't stop him, just let him prattle on, though you *do* allow your mind to wander, to saunter down five miles or so south of here, to where Tina is probably in the bathroom peeing again, which is pretty much all she's done lately because *pregnant women pee a fucking lot*. Chalk that one up to Things Your Mother Didn't Teach You.

———

Here is what Tina would say if she knew your mother didn't approve of her: Fuck that bitch.

———

The guy is *still* talking, so you pull your phone from your pocket, pretend you heard it *bing*, tell him you're very sorry but you've got to take this, put your hand on the car door, and then he's grabbing you by the elbow, telling you to sit here another minute, that he's not done talking to you. "Money in that bag," he says, "least you can do is give me twenty minutes of your time to talk about the future." His fingers dig into your elbow hard, dude's got a grip on him, and of course he does, as he's told you before, he was a quarterback back in his day. He tells you to sit your ass back in the seat, and his fingers dig in a little harder, and you don't think much about it, you just swing hard, knock the fuck out of him, and there's some blood, sure, but you think he probably got off light. Pull that grabby-grabby shit on some of the players on your team, and he'd have been in a coma, but you're not one of them—no skin off your back if he wants to relive his glory days talking to a seventeen-year-old he's bribing— you're just annoyed that he decided to swing his big dick after his mentorship speech. While he's snorting bloody mucus across his button-up and sport coat, you say, "I ain't got a problem with you wanting a conversation after you give me this money, but don't spin me some bullshit about needing a daddy and then put hands on me."

You don't wait for an answer, just grab the sack of cash, clear out of the car, move across the lot. The guy won't say anything, won't call the police to press assault charges, won't tattle on you to your coach or to the coaches at his school because it would only hurt his team if he did, and, after all, it doesn't matter what you do in a car in a parking lot. It matters what you do on a day in February. It matters which school's piece of paper you decide to sign. And you will sign one of those pieces of paper. You have decided that this is a thing that is going to happen, and if by God some other asshole—Tina's dad, Tina's brothers, your coach with his morality pledge—wants to stop you, you'll knock the fuck out of him too. If one thing has asserted itself to you tonight, it is that *you* are the one with the power. You knew this in an abstract way, but now, your knuckles bloodied, the knowledge has become concrete.

You get into your car, start the engine, think about what you're going to say to Tina when you hand it over to her. The guy has gotten out of his car, is starting at you, blood running down his face, rage in his eyes, but you don't get out, don't roll down your window, just turn the key and pull out of the lot.

There is a word you haven't allowed yourself to think, a word that has been needling around the back of your mind from the moment she told you—in the middle of a rant about perfume, mind you—that she was pregnant. You haven't said the word to her, and she hasn't said the word to you, and you haven't even let yourself look at the word in your own mind yet. When she made that confession you felt yourself sliding into a backpedal, felt time extending for you just the way it always does when you're shadowing your man, when you're ready to make a play on the ball, and you reached out to the man in the German sports car, used the card he slipped you when you were on an official visit to Tech earlier in the year, and you arranged the meeting, and you made vague promises, and you took the money, and you punched the guy, and here you are in your car. It is time for the next move, time to drive to Tina's house, to take her to the Mexican restaurant where she will order enchiladas that will probably make her sick and where she will talk and talk and probably drive you a little wild with her talking until you interrupt her by handing her the bag and speaking the word that you have not allowed yourself to speak. In one way or another, you'll feel your whole sprawling future settling in front of you like a ticking clock as you say that one lonely word.

Absence

I.

Laurie keeps crickets. She finds them in the backyard, nestled amid the weeds and leaves, and she puts them in small boxes originally intended for her dollhouse fixtures. She pokes breathing holes in the tops with a small screwdriver and pads them with cotton face wipes and lines them on her windowsill. She slides blades of grass through the openings daily. At night, she can hear the rustle and thrum, which comforts her.

Rachel drinks gin and tonics with a slice of cucumber. She tells anyone who will listen that cucumber is better than lime, that it brings out the gin's floral scent rather than masking it. In the evening, she sits out on the back porch surveying the empty yard. She likes to inhale just before sipping the G&T, to get a sharp noseful of the bitter gin before letting it slip cold between her lips.

Dave cuts deals. His store manager tells him to stop, but he insists. If LSU wins the championship, he says in television spots, circulars, mailers, newspaper ads, your mattress purchase is free. The people who buy mattresses call him "Junction Dave," though no one else in his life does. Junction Dave's Mattress City. He says it sometimes in his office in back, his voice low, muttering the words, feeling the curve of them, understanding their contours in a way he cannot understand other things, no matter how he tries.

Laurie rides the bus to and from school. She sits with her best friend in the back third. Not the back row, but close enough that they can hear the gossip and watch the craziness. Some mornings, a boy will hit another, and they'll tumble into the aisle alongside Laurie and her best friend, and the bus will screech to a halt, and the driver will march down the long aisle to separate the boys. Some mornings Laurie just looks out the window at the trees. She likes all the trees this time of year. Bare branches stark against the lightening sky.

Rachel works again. She sits five days a week at the reception desk of a small law firm. She answers the phone. She plays sudoku on the computer.

The game has a hint button, but she tries not to use it. Rachel likes to slot the numbers into their proper places, likes to see the way a block fills up and is set aside by her mind. The game lets you make three mistakes before it tells you that your win streak is over. Rachel's streak stands at thirty-seven. Thirty-eight.

Dave takes long lunches. He tells his manager to hold down the fort. He chuckles. He slaps the delivery guys on the back as he moves out through the rear exit, past the stacks of mattresses that will eventually go into the showroom or to people's bedrooms. He gets in his car, an Audi he still brags about sometimes when flirting with a customer, and he drives to a Waffle House across town, where he orders his hash browns smothered and covered. He takes his time eating them, and then he drives out to the lake, where he sits and watches the smoke chug from the refineries across the water. Some days, he can see the flare of a fire from a burn-off. Some days, he closes his eyes and sees only darkness.

Laurie always gets home first. Then Rachel. Then Dave. Laurie plays her Nintendo Switch. Rachel fixes her first G&T, which she drinks while Swiffering the hardwood. Dave eats a handful of heart-healthy mixed nuts. Laurie goes into the yard for blades of grass for her crickets. Rachel orders dinner. Dave opens the door when the food arrives. Laurie and Rachel and Dave eat on the couch, at the coffee table. Laurie and Rachel and Dave watch *The Simpsons* or *King of the Hill*. Laurie clears her plate. Rachel clears her plate. Dave clears his plate. Before bed, Laurie drinks milk from a tall glass, drinks it down until it's empty.

II.

Rachel told her father he could relax, could stop worrying, could let loose the reins a little bit. They were sitting on the back porch of his cabin overlooking Black Lake, up near the Arkansas border. He leaned forward, propping his forearms on his knees, his head nearly against the screen that kept the mosquitos at bay. "I just want what's best for you," he said.

"I know that, Daddy."

"You sure you're ready?"

"I love him."

Rachel's father leaned back in his chair, then exhaled loudly. Out in front of them, the sun was dipping low, and Rachel could just make out the shapes of the cypress knees that jutted all around his old wooden pier. The next day, they'd go out on the lake in his little johnboat, would catch a mess of crappie, which Rachel's father would fillet and fry in the little kitchen of his cabin. He would dip his in tartar sauce, and she would dip hers in ketchup, and the two of them would eat in silence, savoring the salty grit of cornmeal licked from fingertips. On this night, though, they talked for a long time about Dave. By the end of the evening, her father nodded his head in the dark of the porch and told her he was proud of the woman she'd become, and they both didn't speak as they cried.

III.

Dave stood at the entrance to the showroom, taking in the empty space. On his hip, Evelyn bounced and squealed. He patted her bottom, told her to calm down. He set her on the carpeted floor, and she toddled off, her body tilting faster than her legs so that every five or ten feet she toppled, caught herself, had to begin the tumbling walk again.

Dave turned to Rachel. They smiled at each other. "I'm thinking 'Dave's Killer Mattresses.'"

"No," Rachel said. "You can't put 'killer' in the name of our store."

"Fair point." Evelyn reached the far wall. She planted her hands against it, pushed herself backward, fell on her diapered bottom. "What about 'Dave and Rachel's Mattress Superstore'?"

"No," Rachel said. "Too wordy."

"A little wordy is good."

"Yes," Rachel said. "But not too much." She walked slowly to the middle of the big room. Dave followed her, and when they were side by side, they sat. Evelyn began the long walk back toward them. "What you need," Rachel said, "is a nickname."

"What kind of nickname?"

"Back in Jackson, when I was growing up, there was an appliance store. Cowboy Maloney's Electric City. Nobody knew Cowboy Maloney's real name. They only knew Cowboy Maloney's Electric City."

"So, 'Cowboy Dave's Mattress Emporium'?"

"No. You can't steal Cowboy Maloney's schtick. Something else. Something just strange enough to lure people in."

"'Friendly Dave's Mattress Warehouse'?"

"No, too easy."

"'Charming Dave's World of Mattresses'?"

"No."

Dave thought for a long moment. He thought about his childhood nickname, Grinchy, and he thought about his college nickname, Roach, and he thought finally about when he met Rachel, about the two of them stumbling half-drunk into the little college bar, The Junction. He'd looked at her, eyes struggling to focus, and he'd said, "Lady, I love you," and she'd punched him hard on the arm and told him to fuck off.

"Junction Dave's Mattress City," he said.

IV.

Evelyn led Laurie to the very end of the pier. They held hands. It was Laurie's first trip to the beach, and though they'd been on the pier by the lake in their hometown before, this pier, a long one that jutted out into the choppy waters of the Gulf, frightened her. She squeezed her sister's hand tighter.

"Look out there," Evelyn said.

Laurie looked down at the weathered boards beneath her feet.

"You're missing it," Evelyn said.

Laurie squinched her toes, felt the sand still stuck in their cracks. She wanted to cry, but she was trying hard to be a big girl, like her sister wanted, so instead, she decided to look. Far out in the water, a pod of dolphins bubbled to the surface, disappeared, bubbled back. "Wow," Laurie said.

"Real dolphins," Evelyn said. "You're going to remember this forever."

V.

Dave and Rachel will divorce out of exhaustion more than anything else. They will drive to the courthouse together one day to file the paperwork, and they will drive back to their house, where Laurie will wait for them. They will all have dinner that evening, none of them speaking of the divorce or anything else of consequence, and then Dave will move into a condo near his store. He will expand his showroom. He will film new ads, ones where he is dressed as an astronaut, a doctor, a cowboy, and he will have Laurie over every Wednesday and every other weekend. They will eat takeout food and Dave will think about the ads as they eat cold enchiladas or cold spaghetti or cold hamburgers. Maybe, he will think, he should get a ventriloquist's dummy.

On those long weekends at her father's condo, Laurie will often think of how clichéd all of it has become, her dad and her mom and her and the lives that they've chosen to lead, but she will not speak these thoughts to her father or her mother. When she finally leaves home for college and pledges a sorority, she'll wince each time someone calls her "sister."

Rachel will date, will stop drinking, will start again, will stop, will manage it and become functional, a good mother for those last years before Laurie leaves. She'll turn to church and then turn back away from church. She will see movies sometimes where people tell other people that the death of a child is unimaginable but that you have to get back to a sense of normalcy, and Rachel will wonder what that means, normalcy, because normalcy would be the opposite of the state she must exist in until the end of her life, normalcy would be something contrary to possibility, and she will grow angry at these movies, will one day hurl a coaster at the wall and then, feeling silly for hurling a coaster at the wall, she will clean the mess, though the hole gouged in the drywall will remain for many years until finally her son-in-law fixes it one day for her, without being asked, but by then she will not remember where the hole even came from, she will only know it was a hole that is now spackled over with putty of some kind that will never match its surrounding paint.

VI.

Many years from now, Laurie will stand with her own child in her backyard, pointing up to a large barn owl in a tree, and she will think again, suddenly, of the dolphins and of Evelyn, and all of the memories will tumble back to her, and she will squeeze her child's hand, and she will wish that her husband had not cheated, had not run off to be with his twenty-something assistant, that he could be here in the backyard with her and with their son, Tim, who is in this moment in the future unaware that he ever even had an aunt, that someone named Evelyn ever even existed in the world. He knows his grandfather, whom he sees once a month or so for Sunday lunch at an old hotel downtown, and he knows his grandmother, whom he calls Maymay and whom he stays with during the days while Laurie works, but none of them have spoken of Evelyn, and he is not yet old enough to ask about her pictures, scattered in family collage frames throughout all of their houses.

Laurie will decide, suddenly, to teach Tim about crickets, and she will lead him to the edge of the grass, will show him how to get on hands and knees and search through the grass for their small, delicate bodies, but in this future moment, Tim will only want to look up at the large owl, which he now cannot fully see in the gathering twilight. He will only want to stare into the dark space in the tree where he thinks its body is. He will focus on the two eyes, glimmering out from all that absence of light, and Tim will know he should be afraid in this moment, huddled on the ground with his mother, who is not looking up into the tree, who is not aware, it seems, of the sharp talons that grip the branch, but instead of fear he will feel a gathering joy, though he is too young to articulate any of this. He will reach out and find his mother's fingers in the grass and dirt, will squeeze her hand, and he will stare into the darkening backyard, and he will begin to know that even in the absence of things, their weight can be felt and measured.

The Somethingoranother's Daughter

Her father was a somethingoranother. In the long, late October or April evenings, he would row out in his boat or drive out in his truck or take the long walk down the shell or gravel or blacktop drive to do somethingoranother, and when he came back wet and cold or dry and hot, he'd lean down and his rough or soft lips would brush her forehead, and she would ask him how somethingoranother had gone, and he'd smile or frown and tell her that she was too young to worry with such matters.

That year, her thirteenth or seventeenth, her father's moods turned harsh or mellow, and as they changed she, too, found herself changing, moving from a stretch of innocence into the realities of the world. In the long or short tumble of years that followed, she would often think back to that spring or fall and how she had learned these turgid or placid messages from her kind or taciturn father, who, in his turn, had learned these things from his own father, who was also a somethingoranother, though in his time (the grandfather's), being a somethingoranother had been more or less respectable than it was in her father's time, and so for her father there was a bitterness or happiness that this fundamental truth of his occupation had changed so rapidly or gradually over the years, and that bitterness or happiness also reached into her.

In that long-past spring or fall, one late afternoon or early morning, she'd sat with her father at the kitchen table or on the porch or in the front seat of his old truck or new car, and he'd reached a hand to her shoulder and she'd said to him, "Do you know that feeling when you are at the very edge of sleep and you hear a door opening across the house and your mind opens from sleep to wakefulness as the door itself opens and in that moment you and the door and the world are moving in tandem? What do you call that feeling, do you suppose?"

"No name for that," he said, and she looked out at the yard or the lake or the dining room.

"What, then, do you call the time after a death, when the person you loved is already buried and the friends have receded into their own lives and you reach for the phone to call the person before your mind has decided to call the person and certainly before you realize that such a thing is no longer possible, when your body is acting on its own rhythms, not yet attuned to the new contours of your world?"

"There's not a name for that, either."

"I guess there's not. But OK. What about when you've adopted a pet from a shelter and you bring it happy-eyed into your home and you work to train it not to piss on the floor or to shit in your bed or to eat your food from the counter before you yourself have eaten it and then, in the lull of days when normality has set in with the animal, you notice that you have grown so painfully attached to it that it has created in you a kind of vibrant longing for affirmation that your discipline has not broken its spirit and you wish briefly that it would eat your pillows and vomit in your shoes so that you can know again the feeling that you felt that first day when it ventured into the space you thought of then as your home but that you think of now as your home, the plural, the cohabited home for the two of you until the animal escapes out the front door one day and chucks itself into the road where it can be devoured by the maw of the world?"

"Not one for that. Any other questions for me?"

She had looked at her father then, as he gazed long or briefly out the window or across the road. He, her father, knew then she would not remember this conversation, would in fact move into the sprawl of her own life which would gradually progress away from him and this time and this place, leaving her eventually a person that he did not know at all, though he had taken part in her creation, and he understood, too, that she would never know him in the way that he was in this moment, and a tear trickled down his bearded or clean-shaven chin, though she did not see it or if she did see it, she did not comment on it. Life does its work, though, doesn't it?

After a time, she reached to his forearm and tugged gently at the wispy hairs and said to him, her voice trembling or calm, "What do you think we should do about all of this?"

Acknowledgments

This collection would not exist if not for the support of my colleagues at McNeese State University, particularly Keagan Lejeune, Jacob Blevins, Scott Goins, Jimmy Trahan, Wendy Whelan-Stewart, Rita Costello, Hillary Joubert, Michael Horner, and especially Amy Fleury, who has supported me and my work in ways large and small and who remains the finest colleague I can imagine.

I owe a great debt of gratitude to all my students but particularly to the fiction students in McNeese's MFA program. Spending my Wednesday afternoons in workshop with y'all wasn't just a lot of fun, it also made me a better writer. You're all brilliant, and I can't wait to read the wonderful things you're writing next. I'm proud to have gotten to talk fiction with you all in Kaufman Hall.

Thank you to Clifford and Lisa Lee Patterson for bringing me to Taleamor Park for a residency that afforded me time and space to work on what eventually became this manuscript. Thank you to my fellow Taleamor residents Dawn Klingensmith, Adrianna Speer, and Stephanie Brownell. Drinks at the next Bird Shirt Day party are on me.

Thank you to the *Virginia Quarterly Review* for a scholarship to their writers' conference. Thanks to John Parrish Peede, Ralph Eubanks, and Allison Wright for the support, and thanks to Richard Bausch for the feedback on my work.

Thank you to Joey Poole and Scott Thomason, who read earlier drafts of this collection and provided foundational feedback.

I owe quite a lot to Josh Canipe, who's read nearly every word I've written since we first stepped foot in Kaufman Hall back in 2004. He's only ever offered the best wisdom and advice.

Many thanks to the editors who originally published portions of this collection. Your support of my work has carried me through.

Big thanks to all of my colleagues at Northern Illinois University, particularly Jennifer Johnson, Sally Blake, and David Walker.

In researching college football recruitment practices for some of these stories, I relied heavily on a network of friends in the online college football community, particularly everyone at Red Cup Rebellion and other message boards that let me tippy-toe around the edges of their world. Y'all are the Marshall jersey pop .gif of people. Steven Godfrey's reporting on bagman and booster culture at SBNation was foundational for these stories.

Thank you to my family, particularly Marilyn Lowe, Eric and Megan Lowe, Marsha and Gary Solomon, Angie Coleman, and Amanda Cotts, who all have supported me and my work in countless ways.

Finally, thanks to Ann, Erin, and Kara, my favorite people, the ones I write for. I love you.

About the Author

Christopher Lowe is the author of *Those Like Us* (SFASU Press) and three prose chapbooks, including *A Guest of the Program* (Iron Horse Literary Review Chapbook Prize Series). His writing has appeared widely in journals including *Greensboro Review, Yemassee, Booth, Quarterly West, Brevity, Third Coast*, and *Florida Review*. He spent a decade teaching in the MFA program at McNeese State University in Lake Charles, LA. Following Hurricanes Laura and Delta, he relocated with his family to northern Illinois, where he is the director for student success for the College of Education at Northern Illinois University. He is at work on a novel.

About the Author

Printed in the USA
CPSIA information can be obtained
at www.ICGtesting.com
CBHW011659040224
4037CB00006B/25

9 781959 569060